The One with the News

The One With the News

SANDRA SABATINI

The Porcupine's Quill

CANADIAN CATALOGUING IN PUBLICATION DATA

Sabatini, Sandra, 1959–
The one with the news

ISBN 0-88984-217-5

I. Title.

PS8587.A2117O53 2000   C813'.6   C00-931780-5
PR9199.3.S155O53 2000

Canadä

Published by The Porcupine's Quill, 68 Main St., Erin, On. NOB 1TO.
Readied for the press by John Metcalf; copy edited by Doris Cowan.
Typeset in Galliard, printed on Zephyr Antique laid
and bound at the Porcupine's Quill Inc.

Grateful acknowledgement is made to the following for permission to
reprint previously published material: Simon & Schuster for selections
from *The Man Who Mistook His Wife for a Hat & Other Clinical Tales* by
Oliver Sacks (Copyright © 1970, 1981, 1983, 1984, 1985 by Oliver Sacks);
the authors for selections from 'Linkage Studies in Familial AD'
by Dr Allen Roses et al.

Every effort has been made to contact copyright holders; in the event of
an inadvertent omission or error, please notify the publisher.
This is a work of fiction. Any resemblance of characters to persons,
living or dead, is purely coincidental.

Represented in Canada by the Literary Press Group.
Trade orders are available from General Distribution Services.

We acknowledge the support of the Ontario Arts Council,
and the Canada Council for the Arts for our publishing program.
The financial support of the Government of Canada
through the Book Publishing Industry Development Program
is also gratefully acknowledged.

2   3   4   •   02   01

for Roger

Who may ascend the hill of the Lord?
And who may stand in his holy place?
He who has clean hands and a pure heart
Shall receive a blessing from the Lord.

Contents

Clean Hands

THERE ARE SIXTEEN windows that don't open in the locked wing of the hospital where Peggy visits Ambrose. The afternoon light stretches down the length of the room where geraniums bloom for the benefit of people who can no longer name the colour red. Peggy goes to visit her husband every other day, taking him clean laundry, banana bread, photographs, letters from Scotland. Ambrose doesn't pay much attention though; he has the air of someone waiting for a train: polite, distant, oblivious. He doesn't notice the part-time staff on the weekend, young people with earrings stapled all the way around their ears, nor does he notice his companions.

Beside him, Maxine hides her baldness with a mesh sun hat even though she has come a long distance from Montego Bay. Her mismatched knee-high stockings slip down her legs below the hem of her floral robe. She has a dignified look, with her hat and bag and her gently arched brows, sitting at the round table with four other patients. Not that she can count to four; not in sequence. One of their group is using her feet to roll herself in her chair forward and back, as if driving a car from Bedrock.

Ambrose eats cubed beetroot and a lump of squash. He has eaten the custard, skin and all, and he has dipped his bread into his coffee and now cannot retrieve it. He looks at Peggy and says,

'You better believe it.'

Peggy is ready to believe anything.

Ambrose came out of the kitchen one night, frowning. Everyone laughed because he was carrying the toaster oven and they thought he was going to use it as a prop for one of his famous jokes.

'A man went out to buy a new suit,' he would say. He had variations of the new-suit joke that might involve the tablecloth, or his bifocals, or Peggy's best friend.

But that night he looked at Peggy.

'I've forgotten how to make the tea.'

This set off a fresh burst of laughter while Peggy went with Ambrose to the kitchen. She put away the toaster oven and told him not to be so daft. She was brisk, bristling around the stove and counters. She got the tray and made the tea while Ambrose stood to one side, watching as though for clues to a game of charades. Peggy took the tray through to the living room, pressing shortbread and cream puffs on her guests. No one commented on the missing punchline; their friends expected odd behaviour from Ambrose. They drank the tea and left crumbs and stained china when they went out into a starless night. Fog muffled the street lights and made their heels echo as they walked to their cars, laughing while Ambrose warned them against the full moon and the neighbourhood vampire. Perhaps when they were safe at home in bed, with the electric blanket turned on low, perhaps then they thought to wonder about Ambrose and the toaster oven and what the joke had been.

But Peggy had known even before the toaster oven, long before Ambrose did. When she'd decided to repaper the bathroom, she went to the discount store and found in a bin exactly what she wanted. She'd walked out of the store without it because it was a 'Shand-Kydd' design and she refused to be bamboozled into buying wallpaper that would benefit the irresponsible mother of the Princess of Wales. Who, in the name of true love – *true lust was more like it* – had left her young family to be influenced by, of all people, Barbara Cartland, while she'd gallivanted through Europe with her lover. On her way back to her car Peggy had assured the absent Mrs Shand-Kydd, most probable cause of her daughter's bulimia and suicidal tendencies, that she would not be getting any of her money. Peggy had gone home, indignant and righteous, only to have Ambrose laugh in her face, walk out of the room shaking his head at her earnestness, her conviction that buying wallpaper out of a bin at the Wallpaper Barn would contribute to the profits of wicked mothers.

'She *left* her children!'

Ambrose thought he was used to Peg's moral indignation. He

was sure Diana had gotten over it, made her peace and all that.

'Oh, you never really get over abandonment, I don't think.'

'No, but it's all over with now, Peg. I think if you like the wallpaper you should have it. Mrs Shand-Kydd has already squandered the money in Monte Carlo anyway. You can't stop her.'

Ambrose got the car keys, bought the paper and dropped Peggy off at the library for the duration of the blitz. Ambrose was an X-acto-knife-wielding terror with wallpaper, an insufferable, wallpaper-hanging perfectionist. He growled at corners out of plumb or, worse, sang hymns off-key as the stuff seemed to fly onto the walls of its own accord. In either case, it was better to keep well out of the way. But when Peggy came home and had a look down the hall, she thought that Ambrose must be having his own revenge on the nasty woman by mismatching her pattern, hanging the jade stripes at tangents to the pink roses. If Ambrose knew, he wasn't saying. He'd been watching baseball since he finished the job, leaning forward in the chair that was speckled with peanut crumbs and salt, and he was furious once again with poor Cito Gaston. It was the eleventh inning with the go-ahead run at the plate. Peggy hadn't mentioned the bathroom. Instead she'd got the little Dustbuster and vacuumed around Ambrose's legs. But the wallpaper bothered her for months while she soaked in the bath, her shoulders knotted against the quarrel of line and colour.

* * *

Peggy turns to help Ambrose sip his tea so that she doesn't have to meet Ken's eye. Ken is sporty. He wears dark horn-rimmed glasses over deep blue eyes. His plaid flannel shirt fits him well and is neatly tucked into khaki chinos. Things have a way of disappearing in the Riverside Health Centre, but strangely, his two-hundred-dollar Bostonian slip-ons have never been stolen. *Fortune* 500 cottage wear. He is not embarrassed to say loudly, 'I just don't know where I can stand.' He levels his handsome eyes at Peggy. 'Can you please tell me where I can stand?'

'I think you're fine where you are, Ken.' In spite of her smile and her firm voice, Ken looks disgusted. It's more convenient to leave him alone, especially since he is across the room from Peggy and won't show his frustration by trying to sit in her lap or putting his head on her shoulder and crying. In this place it wouldn't do to tell Ken not to be so daft.

Lucia concentrates on the cup of tea before her. Her hand, jerking forward and back, gradually makes its way across the tabletop fastened on the arms of her wheelchair to the plastic mug. It doesn't matter if she spills; she is still wearing her backless hospital nightie. Her arms are visible, every sinew and muscle etched in thinness and strain. They aren't able to get her dressed every day. She is aggressive, used to wringing the necks of chickens and rabbits that she gutted and cooked for her family. She hasn't been permitted to wear her upper plate since the night she bit the orderly's ear, and now there's a soft, black gap in her grimace.

She finally reaches her mug of cold tea in one spasm and sends it clattering to the floor of the dining room where it spins for a ridiculous length of time. Lucia grips the tabletop. She pushes and pulls against it. The bolts rattle. She shrieks and cries rhythmically, straining toward some awful crescendo. Peggy wants to slap her. But Ambrose looks at her and shakes his head. For a minute, he is her ally. Her former conspirator.

Maxine offers comfort.

'Now stop cryin'. Ye must not cry like dat. Ye must put ye trust in de Lord and He will deliver ye. A'm tellin' ye no. Ye must jest trust de Lord Jesus and ye must ax him inte ye haht and He will take awa all ye feah.'

She rubs Lucia's hand and begins to sing 'Amazing Grace', which seems to calm her. Peggy thinks about joining in. She has always liked the penultimate verse:

> *Through many dangers, toils, and snares*
> *I have already come.*
> *'Tis grace hath brought me safe thus far,*
> *And grace will lead me home.*

These days she might question what it means to be brought safe this far but she knows about the dangers, toils, and snares. She sits quietly, wiping the drool off Ambrose's chin, wondering why Maxine, so apparently calm and sensible and kind, is locked up on the dementia ward. But Ambrose also seems sensible, and most days behaves in an affable and gentlemanly way. The other days, the ones that sent him here, had their own sickening protocol. When Peggy's feeling sorry for Ambrose, she makes herself remember the time she tried to show him how to open the front door. She remembers his face close to hers, blurring at the edge of white pain. His voice whining in the air above her, above the white pain blasting through her head against the jamb. She makes herself remember trying to drag breath past the swelling vomit in her throat.

* * *

After the problem with the toaster oven Ambrose started carrying a notepad on which he wrote his name, address, and telephone number, as well as instructions for making tea. They joked about his lists and about how he was finally going to succeed at doing errands that he had all his life disdained, but which he now took to with enthusiasm, if not desperation. The conquering of items on the list gave him confidence and so Peggy ignored her fear, watching the man who never wrote down anything before now sit at the table ticking off the moments of his day.

1. go to the bathroom, brush teeth
2. have breakfast
3. post office, buy stamps
4. bank, withdraw $400 #013-27640

'Why are you withdrawing four hundred dollars?'

Ambrose looked at her, his expression contemptuous. Peggy blinked and could not speak.

He said carefully, enunciating consonants with the precision that comes from disgust, 'I am withdrawing four hundred dollars because I want to have coffee with my friend, Alexander Baines.'

Ambrose suddenly heard the sound of his voice and laughed.

They blessed that laughter for days.

Weeks later it became a matter of routine for Peggy to take his wallet when he wasn't looking and remove the hundreds of dollars there which he would otherwise be trying to give to the Second Cup lady for a mug of Colombian Supremo.

* * *

During the war, Peggy's mother had invited Ambrose home from church. He was stationed near Kilmarnock and she felt sorry for him because he was so thin and his ears were enormous. After the war Ambrose sent for Peggy to come to Canada and they were married on New Year's Day. Ambrose said she was his best resolution.

He'd had to pay her passage because it had taken her two years to decide whether to leave her family to marry a Canadian soldier and settle in a foreign country; she had waited too long to be considered a war bride. This annoyed Ambrose who was so certain of everything. He seemed always to live without regret. But it had been a difficult decision and not, as the preacher warned, one to be entered into lightly. Peggy was the eldest of six children, had all but raised her younger brothers and didn't want to leave all she knew for a skinny Canadian who hadn't even taken the trouble to propose in person.

She had taken the ring out of the box that Ambrose's friend presented. It hadn't surprised her that it fitted and that it was lovely. Ambrose was a jeweller; in Canada he had closed up a struggling business to join the air force. Peggy gave the ring back to Eustace, saying she would think on it and would he like to stay to tea.

Sometimes Peggy talks to Ambrose about those days now. On bad days he gives her a shove that bruises her arm but on good days he lets her take his hand and give him a small kiss. Peggy tries to keep him from forgetting what she wants to remember. 'Pride feels no pain,' was her great-aunt Mary's axiom, but Peggy has the uneasy sense that the stiffness between her shoulders isn't new, isn't the result of living with Ambrose's disease, but rather something to do with the way she has always held herself. Sitting beside him she wonders if she all her life pushed him away with the stiff margin of her posture. She pressed starch into his collars and cuffs, turned from his kiss outside the door of his shop downtown. He bought her a nightie for Christmas one year, a sheer, lurid mauve that she thanked him for but never wore. He never bought her another one. These are not the subjects of her reminiscence.

Years ago they had had an infestation of mice who seemed to be living on old sponges under the kitchen sink. Ambrose went to Pro Hardware, bought three traps and set them. In the night, they woke up to first one snap, followed by two others and a great deal of thrashing. Ambrose went down to look after the bodies and Peggy drifted back to sleep.

They slept in late and woke up curled like spoons in a drawer. Ambrose did not make it easy for Peggy to turn around, and for once, she held still, she let the clock tick, and didn't quote from Proverbs, telling him to look to the ant, oh sluggard. He held her against his chest. She could feel the bend of his elbow at her side and his breath in her hair. Her whole backside warm, her feet, too. A pleasure she did not, for once, circumvent. Suddenly, Ambrose got up and pulled on his trousers. In a few minutes she could hear him rattle around in the freezer, open and close the back door before he came back to bed and pretended to sleep.

Peggy waited, watching Ambrose who has a fine profile, until he could no longer stand being stared at. He told her what had happened in the night. Two of the mice were dead but the third was caught by its leg in the trap and was very much alive.

'What did you do?'

'I didn't know what to do. If I let it go it might come back, a peg-legged mouse, for revenge.'

Peggy smiled. 'Well?'

'If I let it go and it didn't come back, some cat would probably devour it, slowly.'

'So?'

'So, I didn't want to smash it.'

'Didn't want to?'

Ambrose was chagrined. 'Well, in fact, I couldn't. Not in the middle of the night.'

'SO?'

'So. I thought, hypothermia might be a nice way to die. Its leg would stop hurting and it would just go to sleep. I put it in a paper bag and put the bag in the freezer. Don't worry, though. I've thrown it out.'

Peggy used to get spitting mad with him during baseball season, when he would leave her. In the same room, three feet away, he could have been on the moon. He sat in the green chair, sternly concentrating, giving advice and shouting 'Hah!' when the team seemed to follow it; shaking his head, disgusted, when they didn't. If she was with him he liked to explain to her.

'They're deliberately walking him.'

'Pull the pitcher! Pull the pitcher!'

'They've lost the game right there.'

She once hurt him deeply by looking him in the eye and telling him that baseball was a game for idiots. The staff at the Riverside Health Centre often turn the game on for Ambrose, but it holds no interest for him now.

When she started to come with him for his regular diabetes checkups, Dr Fortuna paid more attention. He noticed that Ambrose had become sullen to the point of rudeness in his exchanges with Peggy. At times he even told her to shut up or he'd shut her up himself. She said that she couldn't just tell Ambrose he had an appointment to see the doctor, rather she had to invite him out for ice cream and hope to trick him through the doors and up the stairs. Dr Fortuna laughed at Ambrose's recalcitrance, which he was prepared to attribute to perhaps a rough spot in the marriage. The patient's health indicators were acceptable; Dr Fortuna didn't pry.

Peggy came on her own one afternoon. She explained that she had left Ambrose with her daughter, that she could no longer leave him alone in the house because he would accuse her of having an affair if she was gone more than fifteen minutes. Or he would have every pot in the house filled with water, set on the stove and all the heat registers, trying to find a way to make tea. She had so far managed to intervene before any disaster could occur. Then she lifted her blond hair from her forehead to show Dr Fortuna the purple swelling. It was a nasty bump caused, she said, when Ambrose was angry with her for locking the door when he wanted to go out in his underwear. She was clearly exhausted and could no longer cope on her own, she said, with Ambrose's problem. She needed some help and wanted to have Ambrose referred to a specialist. Before she started hitting back. Dr Fortuna gave a memo to his secretary to begin the paperwork required by the Health Centre before it would send a social worker to assess the situation.

Dr Fortuna liked Ambrose, who had been his late father's patient. He thought about the St. John Ambulance course he'd taken as a child. The course his mother sent him to on Wednesday evenings through blizzards and hailstorms so she could choose which of the twelve Wednesdays she might like to sit in the garage with the door closed and the engine running. After learning to make a splint, a sling, to apply pressure to open wounds, to put his lips on a stranger's and breathe, after each of these tasks the instruction was '… and wait for the doctor to come.' Now he was the doctor, bag in hand, with no more clue what to say or prescribe or slice or stitch than he had when he'd come home in March on a Wednesday night and couldn't find his mother.

Peggy learned to sneak Ambrose's tricyclics into his morning orange juice. The doctor had told her that the pills would modify some of Ambrose's most troublesome behaviours. She learned to dodge bullets, to find her perimeters every day. Dr Fortuna's notion of comfort was feeble. He told Peggy not to take it too hard, that everyone has to die of something.

In January Ambrose started refusing to go downstairs at home, but Peggy wanted him downstairs for breakfast and had no time for his nonsense. The VON would take one arm, Peggy the other, and they would pull while he dug in his heels. They slid him in his leather slippers toward the first stair and once he felt his foot on it, down he would go, as long as they held on. He was intense, determined. It was as though he believed that the floor dropped away at the top stair, that he stood on the brink of a jagged chasm opening at his feet.

* * *

When Ambrose's things began to disappear they assumed, the staff and Peggy, that other patients were helping themselves. She didn't ask any further, but she took his watch and signet ring home and put his name on everything else. He kept no money there and didn't seem to miss it.

They called Peggy at home one day to say that Ambrose had had a fall. When she went in his eyes were swollen, shut, aubergine, his nose was broken and bleeding; he'd had four stitches in his brow and two more in his chin. At least two teeth had broken off and the roots would have to be removed under a general anaesthetic. The doctor had asked for nose packing, where was the nose packing, don't you stock any nose packing? Ambrose had answered with alacrity that he had some at home but had forgotten where he had put it. He was happy to see Peggy. There's my girl, he said. It took two weeks for the purple, brown, green, and yellow bruising to dissipate so that Peggy could take him down to the cafeteria for coffee and a Hershey's chocolate. He liked to roll it around in his mouth. He was very jolly. She could see it first in one cheek and then the other; it must have tickled him to have such control.

Peggy cried quietly in her bed that night, although she had no one to disturb. Her mother used to say about most things that happened in life, 'Ach well, there've been greater losses at sea. Just gie yersel a shake, lassie, and go sweeper the carpet.' She had sweepered the carpet, vacuumed it, and then, still dissatisfied, had rolled the whole twelve feet of it herself and hauled it outside to beat. She strained her neck lifting it over the porch railing. She began thrashing the accumulation of dust and dirt. Peggy muttered, encouraging herself, punctuating every syllable with the carpet beater.

'Filthy! Absolutely filthy. And folk think they're clean. How could anything be so disgusting?'

Her eyes watered. She held a tissue to her nose with one hand and pounded with the other until she could no longer lift her arm. She came in sore and shaking and fell asleep.

She dreamt about her children. Alice stood to the left of a store aisle smiling at Peggy who was wrenching Connie's hand, the hand of an infant, so sharply that she dislocated the elbow. The image shifted to the emergency room where she held Connie while the Chinese doctor, who sang 'Country Roads' in Cantonese, pulled the elbow back into place. Peggy objected to the clicking sound that Connie's arm made after the doctor was finished, insisting that the arm was not fixed yet; the doctor must make it right again. He stopped singing to inform Peggy that the arm would never be right again.

* * *

Sitting beside him today, Peggy holds his cold, dry hand in hers. All the facets of her love for Ambrose converge in this permitted touch. Sometimes she sneaks lotion into her palm and works it over his hand, surreptitiously, affectionately. Ambrose hates her to look after him. If she seems to be caring for him he will try to hurt her.

Peggy wants to go out for lunch to the place downtown that still believes in linen, and she wants to go with a friend who isn't trying to be sad. Because of what she calls her 'situation', because of Ambrose, most of her friends only offer her well-intentioned pity. If she goes shopping, if she buys a new sweater, she feels she will have to explain to the generally opinionated and disapproving public of other women. Women who will say, 'Poor Ambrose,' while other women would respond, 'Poor Peggy.' The same women who would feel compelled to say in the next breath, 'She may be poor but I saw that sweater at Holt Renfrew and there is nothing poor about it.' So Peggy will have to admit that she got it on sale, forty percent off and then another forty percent again, and that in fact her friend Louise made her buy it.

Ambrose would have taken her to Pascal's more often if she had let him. The expense was outrageous. She could feed her family for a week on what they charge. He used to have to spring it on her. To call ahead and ask for a menu for Peggy without prices on it. This only made her more suspicious. She went reluctantly, uncomfortably, spoiling the gift with her concern. Peggy's worry about money has fallen to the bottom of the list. She would like to go to that restaurant. They hold the chair as Ambrose used to and they lay the napkin, crisp and white, in her lap. But she would have to go alone and she would have to take a book. She would have to pretend that she is still able to read, to concentrate on anything but the hazards of the next moment. Far too exhausting. And, to her mind, pathetic. Peggy stays home with toast and tea.

She wonders what she will do with his beautiful new suit. Ambrose was so handsome in a suit. Here he wears elasticized trousers for easier changing. But there's nothing easy about it. She knows he is as fierce with strangers who attempt his personal care as he was with her. He looks frail, with his fresh scar and his unfocused eyes, but he has reserves, as his orderly, Gord puts it, of *piss and vinegar*. Peggy thinks he will probably have a few more scars before he's carried out of here. To what? She hopes the scars are because of sinks and tables and not because the nurses have become angry and hateful toward him. As she was.

'Do you hate me, Ambrose? Do you not love me any more?' When it seemed to Peggy that she spent whole days crying she would ask him this.

'Don't be stupid,' he'd say. 'Get up. What're you doing on the floor?'

She wanted to hit him. She wanted to walk out of the house and let him set fire to it, or himself, or the neighbour's cat while he tried to plug the beast's tail into the wall socket and boil it for tea. It was outrageous that she should have to live like this, that something could wreck what had been so carefully built and tended. She wanted mercy. She wanted her prayers answered, her will, not God's done, now. Smartly. She would get up, rub the darkening bruise and say again, a mantra from which no serenity came, 'This is the disease, this is not my Ambrose.'

But she couldn't help wondering. Which was the illusion? The flying years of what she remembered to be affection gone like a camera flash, over before they started, over before she got used to them. What happened to Ambrose's disconcerting love of her body? His jokes about her breasts, his ceaseless interest in them? She remembered the monthly relief of her period. *Peace, perfect peace, for a couple of nights anyway.* Ambrose was always after her, always happy to be close.

'Come on, Peg. Give us a kiss.'

'Ach, Ambrose, I'm trying to finish this letter.'

'This letter?' he would ask as he spilled his tea on it. 'Now that's a shame. Better start again in the morning.'

Although Peggy was certain such moments had occurred in her marriage, moments that made her smile, made her know herself as, of all things, desirable, she could no longer easily remember them. They were all replaced by dreary months before he came here, when Ambrose would hit her. He hated needing her to help him to the bathroom; he hated her for trying to put the Depends on or change soiled sheets or brush his yellowed teeth. She knew it was himself he hated. But it wasn't her fault.

She got so tired of covering up the invisible lady all dressed in black that Ambrose would see at the end of the couch.

'She's so pale,' was all Ambrose could say. He paced and fretted until Peggy got the plaid mohair blanket, the one they brought back from Britain on their silver wedding anniversary, and draped it over her. Then Ambrose would be able to sit down and drink his coffee and eat his biscuit.

* * *

Peggy listens to Maxine. Trust in the Lord. She used to trust unthinkingly. Now she feels she is hanging on by her fingernails and takes some comfort in the words of the Apostle to Christ. *Where else could we go, Lord, for you have words of eternal life?* Where else indeed? *I know that my Redeemer liveth.* Ambrose's favourite: *O for a thousand tongues to sing my great Redeemer's praise.* Ambrose, she knew, had once believed and trusted. Did he still? Coming out of anaesthetic after his heart surgery last year, he had held his arms up in the air, looked at Peggy, and said, 'My hands are clean.'

* * *

'I'm sorry, Peggy.' The brief slip into sense is breathtaking. 'I'm such a stupid old boy, aren't I. But I love you. Don't forget.'

'I know, Ambrose. I love you too. Would you like to get a cup of coffee?'

Ambrose smiles. 'If you have the time.'

Maxine comes over and puts her hat on Ambrose's head. Most of her hair has been torn out; her scalp is bare and scabbed. Lucia has stopped wailing. She has the range of a professional mourner and in spite of dementia, she seems to be keeping in voice. Ambrose is smiling. It's a good day. His bib is institutional green and conceals the striped shirt Peggy laundered and pressed for him yesterday after he tried to use it for toilet paper. The lines and the creases are perfect. The pattern matches. For Peggy, the bib is the quintessence of the institution and the disease. She would like to tear it off and rip it with her teeth and nails and stomp on it, burn it, sift it out of the ash and spit on it. But she sometimes sees Ambrose look at his bib with a gleam in his eyes. As though he were planning something. As though he were going to use it as a centrepiece for one of his famous jokes.

The Light That Fell Behind Him

PINCHED BETWEEN HER FINGER and thumb, Alice's mother's letter dangles above the kitchen table. Alice drops it there with the unopened collection. The stack of letters sits beside her health card and the pre-admission form. She thinks she might take them with her to the hospital when she goes on Friday because she would hate to die under anaesthetic and have her mother find out she didn't even read the lines, never mind what was between them.

For now she won't read these words about Ambrose. She knows her father's disease is made of tangles, knows the tangles don't stop at his skull. She'd rather read words written by people she's never met for whom the knots are only very interesting. Sitting on the couch she is hip-deep in textbooks that won't help her in the morning when she learns to assess young tonsils and give well-baby immunizations. Alice's patients will get measles, mumps, chicken pox. Their parents will insist she rush to emergency to assess their child's swollen arm. When she diagnoses a mosquito bite they will have the grace to seem sheepish.

For months, she has been compiling research for a paper that will never be given, formulating conclusions for a diagnosis that will never be delivered, becoming a secret expert. She takes notes while she reads:

> *Hippocrates introduced the historical conception of disease, the idea that diseases have a course, from their first intimations to their climax or crisis, and thence to their happy or fatal resolution ...*

Resolution, she decides, is a good word, connected as it is to solution, conclusion, decision, settlement. If you didn't think about it you might not realize that what happens in all cases eventually is death. Alice's mother would have approved of Hippocrates. He was so tidy. Alice appears to be a tidy person who knows from long experience at which angle the couch cushions should be set and how to manage the balance of plants, candlesticks, and photographs on the side table to create a nice effect. She can do these things without thinking, with one hand tied behind her back, but Alice knows she is a fraud. She cannot allow guests to hang up their own coats in her closet, or be within earshot when she can't find the wretched shoe she knows is under her bed. Out of sight would be out of mind for Alice, except that she has one shoe and must find the mate. If the coat closet door could be hermetically shut forever, she thinks she might never miss what's been tossed there. Mornings, she stays in bed until the last possible minute, having finely calculated the time it takes to wash and dry her hair, eat a piece of toast. She never reckons on losses and distractions. She turns the page.

The brain is involved in the encoding, storage and retrieval of information. The neurons and glia are the cells involved in these processes and the neuronal synaptic membranes function as the communication centre of the brain.

One of the things in Alice's closet is a dark, expensive-looking dry-cleaner's bag, the kind used for items that have been sealed with some care and finality. No one but Alice knows that inside is the uniform that Ambrose wore while he repaired instruments on the planes that crossed the Channel to drop bombs and spies on enemies. The senile plaques and neurofibrillary tangles lurking in obscure corners of his hippocampus would not be named for another generation. Her mother, Peggy, thinks she gave the uniform to the Sally Ann. The traces of eczema that afflicted him since the war, from the process used to delouse the air force sheets, have been painstakingly removed.

Her father was once a young man: hopeful, prone to practical jokes that endeared him only to some people. He wasn't careful about choosing a victim. Always ready for fun, he thought everyone else was something like him. Peggy likes to say it was the influenza that gave Ambrose an understanding of gentleness. He was laid low in the base hospital, near Kilmarnock, at the mercy of nurses whose uniforms he had occasionally sabotaged by rigging the clothesline to snap under the weight of damp, white linen. Already thin, he lost twenty pounds he could ill afford and all but crawled back to the barracks when he was finished with the vomiting, convulsions, diarrhoea, fever, and bed sores. He was thankful to God for his life. He went to church as soon as he was able and met his future mother-in-law who insisted, ration cards notwithstanding, that this poor boy come home for a decent meal.

If Gran had thought Ambrose was starving then, what would she think of him now? He is emaciated, brittle. Alice's finger and thumb might enclose, if she visits, the space that his biceps takes up. Alice is quite attached to Halifax, to the harbour, the bike trails, the university. She has a lot of work to do. It is hard for her to get away to measure her father's arm.

It is part of their family lore that Ambrose wrote to Peggy every day until she opened her door one afternoon to his best friend. She was frightened something had happened to Ambrose and here was this slight fellow come to break it to her gently. Instead he blushed, took a small velvet box out of the breast pocket of his uniform and asked Peggy if she wouldn't like to marry Ambrose. She said ever after, 'People did odd things during the war; it was no time to balk at a second-hand proposal.' Peggy took two years to finally decide.

Alice's father worked in his store downtown fixing clocks, selling watches and jewellery, sitting patiently behind his counter with the magnification lens fixed on the arm of his glasses, listening to complaints and answering questions. He handled the small gears and jewels deftly, setting them with long tweezers and the lightest graze of oil. Customers who tried to fix their own watches with globs of sewing machine oil made him laugh, and made him money too. On Friday nights Peggy would stay at the store so Ambrose and Alice could go to the Diana for supper. Ambrose liked the banquet burger deluxe, tomatoes, lettuce, mayonnaise and hot mustard; Alice had French fries and rice pudding. The cook gave her extra whipped cream, which Peggy would scrape off if she was with them; Alice had heard her mother refer to her as 'solid' when she was not supposed to be listening. She had stood naked before her mirror, trying to figure out what solid meant and what it could possibly have to do with whipped cream. Now, more than adequately informed about cholesterol, proteins, and complex carbohydrates, Alice still thinks solidity should come from solid foods like roast beef and lamb chops and boiled potatoes, which choked her as a child, and not from something as unsubstantial as chocolate mousse.

Alice loves the words she reads on this sunny afternoon which so confidently delineate the terms of her father's small catastrophe. She turns the page of Yamaoka's study, more sanguine that if the Japanese are on the job the disease will soon be aerodynamic, digitally mastered, inexpensively engineered, cured.

> *Recently, St George-Hyslop et al. mapped the gene for familial Alzheimer's disease (FAD) in a series of early onset Alzheimer's disease families to chromosome 21 ... The mode of inheritance in these families is consistent with autosomal dominant inheritance with age dependent penetrance.*

When Ambrose and Peggy used to visit the small psychiatric hospital near St Thomas once a month, Alice stayed with the next-door neighbour. She picked the flowers that her parents took to Ambrose's sister, who suffered, the doctors said, from pre-senility, the result of hardening of the arteries, arteriosclerosis. Alice was eleven when she first heard that word. She thinks it's why she went to medical school. It was the best outlet for her sesquipedalian proclivities. She rolled the word in the hollow of her mouth, so full and definitive. She didn't know that, among other things, it meant that her aunt did not recognize either Ambrose or Peggy while they talked to her and pushed her chair out into the sunshine. They had removed her from the nursing home where she was left to sit in her faeces, unwashed, cold, and probably hungry, though she never complained, indeed, couldn't complain.

When Ambrose's other sister started punching her docile husband and demanding that he get off her property, and screaming that he was a rapist, thief, murderer and who the hell was he anyway, Alice wasn't supposed to hear. She sat on the landing, listening, while her uncle told Ambrose that he was putting his wife in the Health Centre because he couldn't look after her any more. Peggy and Ambrose visited once a week and ducked when Auntie swung.

The day after tomorrow Alice will get up at 5:30. She'll shower, but she won't put on any make-up. She'll put her toothbrush in the bag that's already packed by the bedroom door. When she leaves, she'll take this book with her. It will help her make sure.

The brain is exquisitely dependent on a constant supply of energy for the survival of neurons.

She likes the word exquisite. Diamonds, pain, truffles. How can all these things be exquisite?

Ambrose's brother started going for long walks. The worst was the night he was picked up halfway to Acton, walking with a swinging, careless gait along the railroad tracks. The police put him into the back of the cruiser, their hands pushing tenderly on the crown of his head so he wouldn't bump it while he wept. Back then Alice was afraid of grown-up tears. Her uncle used to bring her Scotch mints and push her high on the swing. He shouldn't have been crying; he certainly shouldn't have been picked up by the police.

Of course he couldn't learn his lesson. He kept fighting to go out until finally he smashed his wife's nose and when she fell her eye was spitted on the tail of the crystal mouse that he had given her for her birthday. Alice is annoyed that her bent-nosed, glass-eyed aunt sits complacently beside her uncle in the Health Centre during visiting hours, chatting sociably with the staff. She was never any fun; she was always only ballast. She was the one who ought to have been thrown overboard.

The experts in the Health Centre must have been licking their lips at the publications and conference papers such a family would generate; the study of Alzheimer's disease was about to explode. Her uncle and aunts were tested, discussed, cajoled out of whatever bits of reason they had left. The doctors invited the rest of the family in for consultation but Ambrose wouldn't go. One way or another, things would work out. He couldn't be persuaded that tests, meetings, or examinations would be any earthly use. He didn't want to feel like Damocles.

Instead, he played. Alice got postcards from New England, Bermuda, Scotland, all pictures of men in kilts. Her parents came to Halifax for a visit where Alice and Ambrose rode bicycles around the harbour. Ambrose would go downtown to talk to strangers about his faith in Jesus Christ. He dealt with diabetes, angina, gall bladder and open heart surgery with grace and confidence in the care of his maker.

Alice has recently purchased an answering machine. She found the instructions very difficult to understand and had to ask Tom to hook it up for her. The explanation had been inaccurately, but philosophically translated into English from Japanese, with instructions for 'happy connections' and 'wholesome messages'. Tom had laughed and offered her an afternoon of happy connecting, but Alice said she had to study. Tom laughed at that, too.

But he doesn't know much about chromosomes and he doesn't know anything about Ambrose. Alice ignores the ringing phone and turns the page.

> If we wish to know about a man, we ask, 'What is his story – his real inmost story?' Each of us is a singular narrative which is constructed, continually, unconsciously, by, through, and in us – through our perceptions, our feelings, our thoughts, our action, and not least, our discourse, our spoken narrations. Biologically, physiologically we are not so different from each other; historically, as narratives – we are each of us unique.

Alice had left town by the time Ambrose began the frightening process of losing his own narrative. This afternoon, two days' drive away from her parents, from making no difference at all anyway, Alice is finding out that Ambrose's nights must have been a pale sort of black, so that even the darkness lacked definition, when he maybe didn't know his own position. Not in the universe, but whether he was sitting up or lying down or speaking or silent. His confidence must have turned a corner without him, left him shaking, maybe holding on to her mother in the night with a force that would have merely annoyed her.

Alice imagines him shivering under the covers, exposed to bare perception without boundaries, sensing a noise that would perhaps be Peggy saying, 'Ambrose, leave me alone, I'm trying to sleep,' but probably unable to distinguish words. Ambrose would see her open face, feel anguish and anger, and stay quiet.

Would he pray? Would it help? Would he know what it was? Would God be with him? Or would he be abandoned? She can choose which form the drama will take. Opera? As in: *sola, perduta, abbandonata*. Or the New Testament: *Eloi, Eloi, lama sabachthani?* Alice is cold, her fingertips feel cold when she turns pages, her eyes water cold saline.

She imagines him reciting his favourite psalm. Maybe Peggy would roll over, hold him and he would begin to know her, to feel her stroking his shoulder blades. He would relax. Remember something. *The Lord is my shepherd; I shall not want. He maketh me to lie down in green pastures: he leadeth me beside the still waters. He restoreth my soul...*

Her father would be comforted, at least by the rhythm of the psalm, would feel his soul restored, sleep deeply. He would be full of ginger in the morning, ready to see last night as a glitch. The fault perhaps of leftover anaesthetic from his surgery. He would be all right. Ambrose would know God was caring for him. Maybe such nights had prompted his obsession with photography. Maybe he needed little memory boosters, now that he was getting older. He would never believe that he was like his brother or sisters. He didn't wander or punch Alice's mother. Her father believed he knew his own name. She has seen him reach for it ... heard him say, 'It's....' Well, he would know that he knew it. That would be the point.

Good nights would make Ambrose feel that he was over the worst of it. If he had been better read he would have known about dark nights of the soul and that he was just beginning his own. He would have known that the light at the end of the tunnel was only a reflection of the light that fell behind him.

He always said, 'There's better days ahead,' usually after Peggy said, 'There've been greater losses at sea.' He meant heaven and she meant not to think too much about her own small troubles.

Alice tries not to think too much about her own small troubles. She's not getting much sleep; she never eats properly. She lies easily when Peggy asks her these mother-questions. She laughs, talks about the scale in the bathroom and how much she hates it. She likes Peggy to believe that she has a routine, that she thinks about things like watching her weight and saving her money for a vacation and not extra insurance, a lucrative pension for a life she's confident will end in a nursing home of some kind. She's making sure it will be a good one. She doesn't talk about Tom. She doesn't talk about the books she's reading these days.

One characteristic of Alzheimer's disease (AD) is the selective dysfunction and eventual death of large neurons and their synaptic terminals in association cortex, which is correlated with the cognitive impairment in AD patients. This profound neuronal degeneration, although relatively specific, cannot be explained ... Attempts to correct for neurochemical imbalance in the AD brain in ... clinical trials thus far have proven disappointing.

Alice envies them the ability to regard these trial results as disappointing. She envies them their ability to fall asleep, simply disappointed.

Alice never drinks tea, having peed through oceans of it at her mother's house. Standing in her kitchen, she sips sweet espresso and does not think about her own little surgery. She's heard it will feel like she's been kicked in the stomach by a horse. But it won't last forever and when she's better, Alice believes that sleep will come more easily. She's told Tom she's going to her mother's for a couple of days and no, she won't need him to water the geraniums on the balcony.

'Look at them,' she'd said, pointing to the brown leaves and scrawny flowers, 'they'd die of shock if someone actually started to care for them.' He seems determined to hang around, smiling at arm's length. Alice wonders if maybe his father has Alzheimer's disease and if Tom is maybe having a vasectomy on Friday. That would be rich. She moves her books to one side to make room for herself on the floor. She marks certain sections with orange highlighter:

There is always a reaction, on the part of the affected organism or individual, to restore, to replace, to compensate for and to preserve its identity.

In one letter, Peggy had written that Ambrose couldn't stop moving. He walked in the living room and dining room. He got an axe and chopped bearing branches off the apple trees in the backyard. He was suddenly hungry all the time or, rather, he couldn't remember that he had just eaten. Left alone in the house he would fill his jar of peanuts with ice cream and zucchini relish to eat while he rifled the cabinets for more. On her last visit, Alice went with them to a restaurant for his favourite fish and chips, watched her mother sit on egg shells throughout the meal, trying to keep him from putting the vinegar in his coffee and the cream on his French fries. Frayed and anxious, Peggy paid the bill, persuaded Ambrose to get in the car and fasten his seat belt.

Ten minutes into the drive home Ambrose turned to her. 'Where are we going?'

'We're going home.'

Ambrose stared out the window. He had, it seemed, developed a child's mastery at sulking. In his demented state he had become a first-rate manipulator, as though he had been studying the two-year-olds at the mall where Peggy took him for walks.

'What's the matter?'

Silence.

'Ambrose, what's the matter?'

Nothing.

'Ambrose, what do you want?'

Scowl. 'Where'll we go to eat? You know you starve me!'

'We just had fish and chips, Ambrose. Now we're going home.'

'I'm hungry.'

'No, you're not. You can't be.'

'What would you know?'

'I know I just paid six ninety-five for greasy old fish that'll proba-bly send your sugar over the moon. Don't you know you're dia-betic?'

'Where'll we go?'

'Home.'

'I'm hungry. Can't you see I'm starving?'

Alice sat quietly, knowing that Peggy might laugh or cry, but that she would have to give in. Alice knew her as a woman who washed all her windows twice a year and her kitchen floor every week, who had learned from her grandmother that there might be lots of reasons for being poor, for having to stop taking the paper and having to eat rice pudding at lunch because there was nothing else in the house, but that there was no excuse for being dirty. Things were to be done in life as prescribed in the Bible: *decently and in order*. Now Peggy went from Long John Silver's to Tim Horton Donuts in a quest to find a food substantial enough to fill Ambrose's mind. There might be laundry waiting or dust bunnies on the grandfather clock where, Alice had once told her, laughing, you would have to be seven feet tall to find them. Peggy was forced to learn to leave them be.

Alice believes she can be forgiven for staying away, for keeping her father behind a particular door. She doesn't want her mascara to run. She doesn't want to lose her mental faculties as though they were people getting off a bus on the last run of the last day of the world. She doesn't trust the instant of longing; she is certain that when she cooks and eats rice pudding it is simply because she likes the taste. She warms the leftovers in the microwave and returns to the worn place on the wool carpet where she has made a cocoon of texts.

Her textbooks allow Alice to keep her distance. Her surgery will terminate the succession of the disease in her family. It's a good decision. A certain one. Alice is sure she is right. In this she is like Ambrose, but without his charm. There may be only a small chance that a child of hers would get Alzheimer's but she prefers there to be no chance, even if it means no child.

The psycho-behavioural troubles of patients with AD *are such that it is very difficult to keep those patients within the normal family environment. Common sense solutions are often successful but trial and error, patience, and a willingness to try a wide range of options are necessary.*

In spite of his petulance and his occasional threats, the things Alice tried to warn her of, Peggy always believed that she would be able to look after Ambrose, that he would never actually hurt her, that the love they had shared for going on forty years would never leave his consciousness. But to all appearances, that was what had happened. Alice knew there was, there would be, no help for it. He became almost belligerently incontinent, flailing at washcloths and having to be skidded and shoved toward a hard, slick bathtub. No wonder he fought. The sides were cold, the tub itself, bottomless. Filled with hot water that scalded his skin, made his breath short and shallow, scraping in his throat. He must have hated it. It must have looked like death. Peggy pushed harder; Ambrose stank. He was filthy. She would make him clean or die trying. At Alice's urging, Peggy joined an Alzheimer's support group and started seeing the Health Centre social worker whose task was to support the primary caregiver and teach 'coping strategies', the gossamer that Peggy clutched.

Alice knows about misery at second hand. Things changed every day for her mother, whose misery would have been easier to live with had it been constant. But Ambrose couldn't be constant. Sometimes he woke up in the morning and said, 'Hello, darling.' They would go for a drive, hold hands, watch *Wheel of Fortune*. Peggy would laugh later on the phone with Alice, who knew there were other nights, when Peggy would go into his room to check him only to be driven back out, gagging on the smell of excrement, which he'd been trying to hide under the pillow, behind the curtains, and in the dresser drawers. She washed sheets every day and she washed Ambrose too in anger and tears, shaking, determined. Finally the doctor ordered home care for Ambrose so a sturdy VON would help keep him clean. Raised on the strict authority of the King James Bible, Peggy had never danced in her life. Now she felt trapped in an awkward and unreliable quadrille, in turn and counter-turn and stand, where she and Ambrose both were always losing count.

Alice didn't know how bad things were. Peggy never mentioned the bruises and always laughed off the threats that Ambrose sometimes made. One night when she was trying to get him ready for bed, he suddenly turned and kicked her in the diaphragm, knocking the breath out of her chest and the back of her head against the wall so that for a few minutes, she lost consciousness. Then everyone found out and even the social worker was impressed by the extent to which Peggy had been able to dissemble. Alice flew home and went with Peggy's worker to complete the forms, admitting her father to the Health Centre where he remains today a well-dressed and pressed gentleman. He is losing the ability to speak or eat; he's forgetting how to open his eyes. Alice hasn't seen him for months. Seeing her father makes her cry more than not seeing him does. And she has never seen the way his shoulders extend like ball joints from which stick-arms dangle. She stays alone on the east coast, her period of residency in paediatrics almost over. She doesn't think she'll move back, though she misses her mother, though she wakes up in the night paralysed, having dreamt about a future.

Alice knows her mother is just lonely, perhaps no longer sure there have been greater losses at sea. She's busy with the support group and the ladies' auxiliary and the women's missionary meeting. She's had deadbolts installed on the doors, which she fastens securely every evening.

Alice worries when she gets left and right confused. She reads, she takes notes, she waits for Ambrose to get pneumonia or cancer or an aneurysm. She waits for God to remember a mercy He used to dispense with more prodigality.

Ambrose Dreams

AMBROSE DREAMS that he's being lifted out of murky, moving water and left on a broad bank of clipped grass that pricks his wet skin. He feels the water and muck leaking from his shoes and clothes, the sediment, twigs, leaves, and tadpoles from the river dribbling back down the bank to its source. He is rescued and brought to a broad place. He feels the breeze and knows his name.

In Peggy's dreams Sean Connery is the bad guy who wants to kill Ambrose and marry her. She has to choose between her husband, Ambrose, whom she's been married to for forty-three years, and Sean Connery. The choice is complicated by the fact that if she chooses Ambrose she chooses death. Death with Ambrose or life with Sean. Because Ambrose buys her carnations, a dozen pink ones with baby's breath, seven ninety-nine cash and carry, she chooses to die with Ambrose rather than live in sin and betrayal with Sean.

When Ambrose lies down for forty winks he ruins Peggy's swaddled bed linen. He takes off his pants and lays them over the back of the chair. He pulls the mohair throw over his legs and puts his head on the pillow. He composes himself for sleep, folding his hands across his chest and taking a deep breath, as though he were about to dive. When Ambrose dreams he moans and winks and twitches like a Labrador retriever dreaming of plump rabbits. Watching him you can see he's on to something. His hair's a mess from tossing around and there are two vertical folds of skin between his tightly closed eyes. Suddenly these will disappear and Ambrose will laugh in his sleep.

Ambrose dreams of hands. His own are finely formed, hairless, pale, and meticulously clean. He was a watchmaker before he started losing his mind and he spent hours looking through an illuminated magnifying glass, adjusting the gears and jewels of watches, fixing the bezel on diamond rings, replacing weights and springs of antique clocks. His fingers always seemed large to him. He kept the nails clipped and filed when he repaired the Bulovas and Gruens and Seikos. The glass magnified any small bit of dirt, crumb of toast, flake of dandruff. His annoyance was manifested in pursed lips and severe humming if, in the middle of close work, he was suddenly distracted by fingernail muck. He would have to put everything down gently, rubies, solder, crystals, and pick away at minuscule filth until he was satisfied. At the hospital before his quadruple bypass surgery Ambrose was sedated and dreaming of the requirement of hands. The anaesthetist came to do his pre-op check and was shocked when the unconscious man beside him lifted his arms and announced, 'My hands are clean.'

On Sunday afternoons, after church and after the dishes are done from the roast beef, mashed potatoes, gravy, squash, beans, broccoli with cream of mushroom soup and onion rings, beets, carrots, fresh rolls, and grape juice, since it is the Lord's day, a day of rest, Peggy will often lie down on the living-room couch. She reads *Decision Magazine*, and doesn't hear the ticking swing of the pendulum or the Westminster chimes that sound the quarter hours. Instead she sleeps. In Peggy's dreams, her rightful home, the land that she and Ambrose will inherit, is in the Northwest. Pristine and cold, it waits for them. Sean Connery wants that land in the Scottish Highlands, which Peggy has never seen. He wants it so badly that he's plotting Ambrose's death. Peggy knows she is in Scotland and it's the eighteenth century in her dream. She knows this and she knows their tartan. It's orange and green and brown and white, the plaid that Ambrose wears. A dangerous thing to do in the years after Bonnie Prince Charlie, when to wear the plaid or play the pipes could easily get you garrotted.

Ambrose has animal dreams. He dreamed there was a cow behind the piano. He made Peggy get out of bed and help him push the piano away from the wall. 'There,' he said. 'Now where will you hide?' Apparently this discouraged the cow, which never returned. He likes the cat dreams much better, though the cat is more difficult to find. Sometimes it hides in his workshop underneath the bench where the dark is thick with spider webs and the dried carcasses of old spider dinners. Once in his dream he knew the cat was in the tool shed behind the lawn mower. He sat up in bed, certain that it was out there and would spill gasoline and he and Peg would die horribly. Peggy found Ambrose standing in the backyard in his underwear.

'Ambrose!' she said, not being one to worry about the wisdom of waking a sleepwalker. 'Are you out your mind?'

'Beautiful evening, don't you think, Peg? What are you doing out of bed?'

'What am *I* ...?' Peggy turned and went back inside. 'Freeze to death if you like.'

God's purpose for cats was never clear to Ambrose, nor was Peggy's insistence that they have one. It wasn't as though they took the thing to the vet or even looked after it much. It stayed out all night and when they went away camping, Peggy would blithely put it outside and ask the neighbour to make sure there was always water in its dish. The presence of a cat brings out the worst in Ambrose, a man not normally given to cruelty. He pokes at them, pulls their tails, makes loud sudden hissing sounds to scare them from their curled sleep. He doesn't like cats. He dreams that there is a cat hiding in the house. He has to find it. If he does find it he gives it a good swift kick. Ambrose is bigger than the cat.

In Peggy's dreams Ambrose is prepared to take the risk of wearing the plaid. Looking to the Northwest, to heaven, you might say, Ambrose prepares to play the pipes, wearing his outlawed kilt and sporran and standing on strong legs, not on the thin, pale sticks that diabetes has left him with. Sean Connery watches avidly as Ambrose bends to one set of pipes of the two laid out on the grass beside the lake. Ambrose positions himself between the onlookers and the pipes, checking the fit of the drones. The other set belongs to Sean, who can barely stand still, whose concentration is exquisite. In a minute he'll be twisting his kilt. He's poisoned his own blow pipe and put it into Ambrose's pipes. In Peggy's dream, she knows this to be true. She knows what it all means, knows it's against the rules of the dream itself to yell a warning, or whisper one.

In real life, Ambrose not only can't play the pipes, but he and Peggy both hate the sound of them. Ambrose's parents were the children of Scots immigrants. He has the heritage, but not the inclination. He thinks kilts are ridiculous. He says about men who wear them, though not in their hearing, 'Ooh, fly away, ye wee fairy,' and he says it with a put-on Scottish burr. Peggy doesn't know why she has this dream. She doesn't like bagpipes and she doesn't care about Sean Connery one way or the other. Her feelings about Ambrose are much less neutral. She has always loved him, but since he got Alzheimer's, sometimes she hates him, too.

When Ambrose was in the war he had eczema. He had to stay in the base hospital, his hands swathed in bandages to keep him from flaying himself. On top of that he got influenza. He spent what seemed like days on a bedpan. He remembered the arc his pelvis had to make on the unyielding mattress to accommodate the pan underneath. Sometimes at night he dreams about the hospital. He dreams that his stomach is cramping, that he is sweating and nauseous and that he can feel the cold enamel framing his buttocks. He doesn't have to strain. Corruption pours out of him, influenza and life leaking away to be tidied up by the young nurse. When Ambrose wakes up these days and sees that he has missed the pan he tries to clean the mess himself with things that are handy, the curtains and clothing and doilies near his bed. He's confused in the dark of his room, uncertain about time and space. He notices that his hands have no bandages so he steals the chance to scratch his armpits and groin where the terrible itch flames. Only there is no itch. No bandages and no pan. Forty-five years since he needed them, but he can't figure that out either. Peggy wakes up choking. She doesn't know about his dream. She just knows if she murders Ambrose now no jury in the world will convict her.

In Peggy's dreams, Ambrose walks past her, past the crowd gathered near the castle. In her admiration of the smart swing of the pleats as Ambrose walks she forgets the danger. She knows the measure of his gait. She sees the calm in him and feels calm herself. In her dream the crowd becomes quiet. They are in the presence of the walking dead. Ambrose, in a tartan, about to play the pipes. People are holding their breath. Never mind that the reed is poisoned. Ambrose might as well take his skeindubh and stab himself through the heart. He's as good as dead.

Peggy's dreams have sound and colour. And history. Location, topography, plot. She can't love Sean Connery, or marry him. She's loved Ambrose since she was a girl. Ambrose stretches his arms over his head and limbers his fingers before he takes up the bag and the pipes. She watches him put the blow pipe in his mouth, tuck the bag under his left arm, and swing the drones onto his shoulder dampening the pipe with his tongue. Laughing with the man beside him, blow pipe held between his teeth, Ambrose takes a deep breath and fills the bag with air. He is peaceful. A level green gaze. His hair is grey in Peggy's dream even though in real life Ambrose's head is still covered in fine, jet-black hair. In Peggy's dream Ambrose is taller. He plays the pipes. For miles in that still evening the sound carries. You would think, dreams Peggy, that the sound moves all the way to London and the throne itself. If the poison doesn't kill him, the English will. Peggy waits and listens to the keening beauty of Ambrose's song. It's as though he is playing a spell. Even the nasty glint in Sean Connery's eye has begun to glisten.

Ambrose often wants to know what is happening. In his dreams he asks the people he knows and the strangers. When he's awake he puts the question in his eyes and looks at Peggy. There was the question. There. He doesn't know what thinking is. Ambrose doesn't know his brain is in serious trouble, that the complex business of circuitry, electric impulses transferring information easily, swiftly is, in Ambrose's brain, becoming a tangled mess. The synapses shift and freeze, shatter like Venetian crystal. Dreaming is better. In dreams Ambrose moves across the Speed River on skates. He glides with his sister who, in the cold air, is sniffing wetly. 'You can't keep that up,' he says and he skates away, barely hearing her tell him not to be so disgusting. He laughs. Ambrose likes jokes about bodily functions. He used to like to spice up the after-church fellowship time by asking newcomers if they'd read the inspirational bestseller, *Golden Streams*, by I.P. Standing. Now he has other questions he would like to ask.

In Peggy's dreams Ambrose doesn't die. Every piper knows his own pipes. The tape of her dream rewinds; she revises disaster from the horizon. She watches Ambrose examine the pipe, see that it has been stuck in askew, hastily it seems. She sees, even as he does, that these are not the marks left by his teeth. Somehow the pipe with those familiar indentations got in the wrong instrument. She watches him shake his head, and switch. She can see him wondering how that could have happened, and then sees the thought itself sink like a penny in a pond. Gone and useless. Ambrose has wind and pipes and hope for Scotland and for the Northwest. He plays.

History doesn't change, isn't changed by Peggy's dream. She might be fey. When she dreams, even when the dream is part of history, there are smells and sounds and texture, continuity and hope and fear and love. Sean Connery is enraged by Ambrose's failure to die. He has a back-up plan. Peggy observes him bend to the rock beside him and lift a small cask, green and jewelled, blown of precious glass, ancient and sinister. He lifts it over his head and smashes it on the scree beside the lake. As Ambrose plays, a bellowing cloud of noxious green gas moves toward the crowd, most particularly toward Ambrose. Peggy is the only one who seems to be aware that it is death moving toward them all. The wind shifts with the changing skirl of the pipes. It blows down from the northwest highlands and dissipates the greasy cloud. Again, no harm is done. Ambrose plays. The evening breeze blows and poor, cranky Sean dies of apoplexy. The English don't come. The people enjoy the music, move closer to one another, breathe in accord. Peggy goes home to bed with Ambrose.

Ambrose's dreams are a lot like his life, now. He remembers driving his car. He remembers addition and subtraction. He remembers that things have names. He tells Peggy to put the light out. When she tells him the light is already out he lifts his hand to slap her. He doesn't remember loving Peggy. He doesn't remember wooing her. Ambrose dreams rather straightforwardly that Peggy is his jailor. That she has keys, large clanking black ones, that could unlock the shackles that wrap around his head and neck, but she refuses. In his dreams, Ambrose hates Peggy. In his dreams he knows who she is; she is his enemy. She has robbed him of his car keys, of his money, of his claim checks for film processing. She puts poison in his food. She scratches him with her nails. She screams at him. When Peggy cries in Ambrose's dreams he knows why and he's glad. When Peggy cries in Ambrose's life, he doesn't know why. He doesn't know why she is a persistent force in his life. She keeps turning up, putting clothing on him, putting her lips to his face in a way that is utterly repugnant. She has, whoever she is, no sense of dignity or restraint.

Collecting

THE PAPER BOY climbed the flagstone steps to the wide front porch. His paper bag was slung across his shoulder, empty except for the cards and the hole punch. He took the bag with him so his customers would know he was at their door on business, so that they would recognize him even though he had been delivering the paper to these people for almost a year. He checked the date twice to make sure he could tell Mr McLean exactly what was owing. Stephen hated collecting. It felt like asking people for money.

Idiot. It *is* asking people for money.

I know, but it's *my* money.

He had this conversation with himself every two weeks. Stephen delivered the paper every day, on school days before five and on Saturdays and Sundays before nine in the morning. No sleeping in. No cartoons. He saved almost all the money except for what he absolutely had to spend on cherry blasters and collecting Leafs and Jays cards. He wanted a drum set, the electronic kind that he could use with headphones in the basement. Then his mother couldn't hear him practise. He didn't have to worry about his father hearing him any more. But the good part was that nobody would know how bad he was until he got good.

But first he had to get money. Lots of it. So he had to knock on doors. He had to collect. It made people mad. Like they thought the paper should appear magically and free. Not everybody. The Sunarthas were always ready with the money. They kept it in a desk drawer right by the front door. Six-sixty a week. They paid him seven dollars and always said, when he went to make change, 'That's okay.'

The Millers were never ready. Their teenage sons, boys older than Stephen, had the gristly parts of their ears pierced. One had a piercing under his tongue and Trevor, the youngest, had one that seemed to connect his eyebrows. All that metal didn't make them smarter.

Trevor, two years older than Stephen, was the only kid in grade eight who still didn't know the national anthem. He only sang it if the teacher was watching him. Somebody told Stephen that if you stood close enough you could hear him singing, *'We stand on God for thieves.'*

'Collecting for the *Chronicle*.'

'Oh,' Trev would answer. 'Oh.'

So you said, Neanderthal. Stephen wouldn't say this out loud unless he was far enough away for a good head start. He was slight and unpierced. Fast, but nerdy.

'Um.'

Stephen waited. Trevor wiped his nose on the back of his hand.

'Yeah.'

Trevor slouched toward the kitchen, stopped and turned.

'My mom's not home.'

'Okay. I'll come back tomorrow.'

And tomorrow, Stephen would have the same conversation only with a different brother. Finally, Mrs Miller would send one of the boys down the street to Stephen's with an envelope that included a good tip.

Phil, the oldest, would say, 'This is from my mom. It's for the, ah ...'

'Paper?'

'Yeah.'

'Thanks.'

'She said she's sorry you had to wait.'

'That's okay.'

'See ya.'

'Yeah.'

Stephen thought they must all use dope. He thought it was funny that Mr Varsky spent ages in health class talking to them about drugs. Big red circles with the diagonal line through the needle or the joint or pills or a bottle of glue in the middle. Like that would stop the Millers. *Oh no! It's the circle with the slash.* Are you kidding? They were probably getting some good ideas, if their conversation was anything to go by. Maybe they sniffed stuff while they were watching *Who Wants to Be a Millionaire?* They sat on the front porch all summer long. Nobody in Stephen's neighbourhood sat on the porch. Nobody hung out laundry. Nobody had dog shit all over the lawn. Nobody repaired their cars in the driveway. Stephen's mother called them the *deliverance people* when she drove past in the Lexus. His mother always waved. Mrs Miller waved back, but the boys, Stephen could see, would be left squinting, trying to figure out who he and his mother were, though they'd been neighbours all his life.

They had an above-ground pool.

Most of the people on Stephen's paper route paid in advance at the office for their subscriptions. They paid the paper direct so all he had to do was deliver. It cut into his tips, but he liked the peace of mind. He had gotten his collecting list down to six customers. People who sometimes hid when they saw him coming up the walk. Like he couldn't see through clear glass. Like he didn't know Oprah Winfrey's voice when he heard it on the other side of the fibreglass curtains. He tried to keep all his customers paid up. His boss at the paper told him that if anybody owed more than twenty bucks Stephen was supposed to call it in and stop delivering. But he hated that. It made the customers mad and then they didn't give him tips and then the drum set seemed more ridiculous.

To give himself courage he visited the used drums for sale in Kelly's Music downtown. They were electronic, flat black discs that could sound acoustic if he wanted them too. One for the high hat, the crash-and-ride cymbals, the bass, the toms, everything. He knew that real drummers didn't respect them. He knew that even if they were programmed for acoustic they wouldn't give him the variations from hitting different parts of the skins. He had tried them. He sat behind them in the store and tapped away without plugging them in. All he could hear was the bop of the sticks, like he was beating on hard rubber. The clerk left him alone for a while and then said it was annoying, told him to leave if he wasn't going to buy. He was going to buy. Just not then. But he didn't want to argue with a guy who looked like he'd listened to way too much Metallica.

He loved percussion. Stephen loved the feel of his bones vibrating. He liked putting his feet on train tracks. He liked to stand close to the curb at the Santa Claus parade when the marching bands passed. He tried to pretend it was all very amusing. After, he and his friends went back to Chris's with their parents and their parents' friends. Sometimes forty or fifty people crammed in eating shrimp rings and *fois gras* and drinking cider or Scotch or wine or hot chocolate or coffee. For kids there was a table full of cookies and brownies and potato chips, all you could eat, whatever you wanted. The house was huge, three stories, with everyone, adults and kids spread out all over the place. Nobody keeping tabs, which was both good and bad. Stephen avoided the waves of laughter coming from the parents and the hisses and slamming doors coming from Chris's sisters' rooms. He and Chris headed out to the driveway to practice slapshots against the garage door. The ball would slice off the stick and slap the metal door. It was old and the hinges were loose so the reverb was great. He wondered if he would be able to make his drums sound like India rubber balls blasting off a bad Sears garage door. That would be cool.

He used to beat on pots till his mother took them away and reduced him to Tupperware. When he was eight he sold his train set to his cousin and bought what he believed was a real drum set, two small toms, a bass and a cymbal. He tried to learn music, but he couldn't make the dots equal sound in his head. It was like trying to make letters on the page equal talking when he was little. He gave up on music. He went for sound. Lots of it. Cut the sleeves out of his T-shirt and pounded. Within a week he'd bashed through the cheap plastic skins and his mother pitched the drums out on garbage day in a big green bag.

Stephen used to like collecting from Mr McLean. He used to say, 'Stephen, fella. Come on in till I find you some money.' Then he would tell Peggy to give the poor lad a piece of shortbread or cake or something.

'Something to keep body and soul together.'

Stephen was amazed at first that Peggy was always able to

produce baking. She would say, 'He does look that famished. Just let me see my tins, till I see what I can find for ye, Stephen.' She meant cookie tins and she generally kept four of them stacked with maca-roons, oatmeal cookies dipped in sweet chocolate, marshmallow rounds with coconut, chocolate-chip cookies. She would select a sampling and offer it to Stephen on bone china with a napkin set on the hall table while Ambrose dug up the money from his pockets.

Stephen was used to Oreos and Chips Ahoy. He usually got home before his mother and helped himself. If the cookies were big enough that he had to bite them instead of popping them into his mouth whole, he ate over the sink so the crumbs wouldn't go on the floor. His mother went ballistic about crumbs. It never occurred to him to use a plate. Stephen's mother came home tired from work. She took the bag of French fries and chicken fingers out of the freezer and spread them on something she called a cookie sheet, which as far as he knew had never seen cookie dough. She nuked the bag of vegetables and opened the bag of salad. She called herself the bag lady and they laughed and ate dinner. Peggy made her own fries from potatoes. Stephen had them once when he was out collecting and interrupted the McLeans' dinner. She insisted that he sit down and have *a wee plate* while Ambrose got his wallet.

Ambrose made a big production of looking for money behind couch cushions, under the hall mat, and in the plant stand. Though he believed he was too old, Stephen couldn't help laughing.

'You never know where Peggy's going to hide the money next. She's quite Scotch, you know.'

'Och, Ambrose, don't be so daft. Just pay the poor lad and let him get his work done. His mother'll be waiting on him coming for sup-per. Isn't that right, Stephen?'

'That's all right,' Stephen would say past the mouthful of cookie. And Ambrose would stand behind Peggy from across the room, hands on hips, head wagging, lips silently scolding. He would make fun of Peggy behind her back, mock her gestures with his eyes crossed and lips all screwy. He looked so retarded. Stephen would slap his hand over his mouth and crumbs would shoot out his nose.

'Ambrose! What are you doing?'

'Nothing.'

If Mrs McLean knew what he was doing, she never let on.

It was fun going there. Stephen never knew what to say after he said, 'Collecting for the paper,' and then told the people what they owed. But he felt nice there. Warmed from the fire and the fuss and the lamps glowing at all corners of the living room.

That was last winter. The McLeans stopped the paper for a while when they were away in Scotland and when they came back, Stephen had a harder and harder time getting his money. If Peggy was home she smiled and paid him and since this seemed how things should always have been, Stephen tried not to notice that he wasn't invited in any more. If Peggy wasn't home he would stand on her porch while Mr McLean looked for money. He rattled the change in his pockets. Pulled some out, but not six dollars' worth. Through the door Stephen saw him look in envelopes on the counter. In the little china pitcher on the bookcase that was full of odd keys and screws and pennies. That was where they kept the punch card for Stephen to punch when they paid him. Ambrose gave him the card but not the money. Mr McLean wasn't smiling. Stephen stared, trying to get the joke. He thought he must look like Trevor.

'That's six sixty, Mr McLean.'

Ambrose stood looking at him. Stephen didn't know what to say.

'It's six sixty, Mr McLean. You know. For the paper.'

Ambrose took out his wallet and gave Stephen two ten-dollar bills. Stephen had change ready in his hand, smelling of sweat and newsprint and copper. Ambrose had dropped his hand, he was't holding out his hand to take the money. Stephen's feet were itchy. His face, hot. He must be an idiot. He couldn't make himself understand.

Mr McLean said, 'Well, then.'

'Here's your change.'

Stephen reached past Ambrose and put the money on the shelf. He had to take a whiz and he had to get out.

He thought he must have farted a bad one or eaten too many

cookies last time before they went away. Or didn't say 'thank you.' These people went to church. He should have used better manners. Stupid.

The last time he went collecting, Mr McLean invited him in. Peggy wasn't around and Stephen stood tapping the punch against the inside of his *Chronicle* bag. He watched Ambrose look for money. He watched him stare back, looking at Stephen and at the blue carpet and at himself, not able to move, but looking like he felt he ought to. That there was some action he ought to be collecting himself to perform. He picked up the punch card and seemed suddenly to understand. Ambrose asked him what he owed.

'I'm sorry, but it's nineteen eighty.'

'What?'

'Nineteen eighty.'

Stephen could hear the furnace clicking on. There was a duct underneath the floor where he stood waiting and if he shifted from one foot to another, he could feel it bend under his weight, could hear it tinny in his ears like the pop of a mason jar lid. He felt the hot air blowing from the vent beside him. He looked at the floor, at his runners, at the place where the sole was separating from the shoe. The laces were grey and ratty. He'd tied them loosely and left them hanging through the winter and muddy spring. The shoes were already almost worn out, already almost too small. Soon his mother would drive him to Runner's Pick and hand him over to the staff.

'He needs shoes. Again. About a size, what would you think, Stephen?'

'I don't know.'

'We'll get him measured, ma'am.'

Stephen's mother was not like the other mothers. She didn't own track pants or any T-shirts with watercolour flowers on them. She hated chintz. And hearts. And welcome mats. She hated to be called 'ma'am.'

'Thank you very much, *junior*.'

The clerk, a new one with a headset around the top of his spiky hair, looked at Stephen who thought this one seemed like he might not figure it out. The smart ones didn't call her *ma'am* again. She preferred to be mistaken for Stephen's big sister, which, her friends told her, she could almost pass for. Big sister from a previous marriage, thought Stephen. Way previous.

After he picked a pair his mother would pay with the Mastercard. It was his father's account. He paid for anything Stephen needed. His mother's pleasure was to buy Stephen top-of-the-line Nikes at two hundred bucks after the sale was over. Stephen's dad never, as far as he knew, complained.

Soon he would get new shoes. There was no fun in it really. Probably if he phoned his dad, he could get the drums tomorrow. But he didn't want anybody else involved in the decision. If he lost interest in two weeks, he didn't want anybody to be able to talk about what a waste of money, and did he think they were made of money, or that money grew on trees, or about the poorhouse, or bankruptcy court. All the things their parents had said to them, which they probably vowed they would never say to a kid of theirs, as Stephen often did. And if he got good at the drums, he wanted it to be only because of him, some sign that whatever happened, he could take care of himself. Whatever they decided to do. Rich or poor.

Right now he was poor and he was waiting for Mr McLean to pay him and he wanted to quit the paper forever and ever and never ask anyone for money again.

He looked up. Mr McLean's eyes were squinting and wet. His face was red.

'*This is completely unacceptable!* What kind of a business are you running, sir? That you let your accounts get so out of hand. You should be coming to collect more often.'

'Well, I come, but you're not home.' Stephen didn't want to say that just a few days ago he saw Mr McLean through the window, sitting there, just not answering the door.

'Watch your language, fella.'

Stephen knew his mouth was open.

'Don't stand there gaping. Move off, now. What are you doing, standing there? Dumb kid.'

Stephen stood about chest high to Mr McLean. He was staring past Ambrose at the grandfather clock. It wouldn't have been hard for him to look up and see his eyes, but he didn't do it. There were things in Ambrose's face that Stephen wouldn't see. Mr McLean's eyes, for example, which had tears in them while he tore a strip off Stephen, as if somebody else was working his mouth and he didn't really want to be talking at all. Or his mouth twisted so mean with black, patchy stubble around it. Where was Peggy? He wondered about the cookie tins. If she still kept them full even though she didn't seem to give cookies away any more. Ambrose had changed into something that Stephen remembered living with, something with lips stretched tightly over dry teeth, with breath blowing down on him like the pockets of gas you hit when you're digging with the floss at the back of your mouth. This, too, was so close to what he had been used to that he didn't for a long time think that Ambrose had gone strange, down a strange road that he himself did not recognize or perceive.

Stephen left. Something was making his eyes and his throat hurt. He pounded his feet on the wet sidewalk until his shins were aching. He finished collecting and went home to change his T-shirt. It had a sour smell and he threw it in the laundry hamper. The magic laundry hamper. That's what his mother called it.

'All you have to do is scrape your filthy maggoty raggedy clothes in the wash and they come out of that magic hamper fragrant and folded. Bearable to human olfactory and visual mechanisms.'

His mother talked funny.

She had started telling him to wear deodorant. She handed him some Speed Stick and said, 'Stephen, it's time.'

'Can I drive now, too?'

'Do you want to talk?'

'Talk?'

'You *know.*'

'Not yet.'

'Any wonderful and amazing changes?'

'Mom.'

'Early morning difficulties? Inexplicable stiffness?'

'*Mom.*'

'Strange hair?'

He didn't think any of his friends' mothers asked them if they were growing hair down *there*. Maybe it was because she didn't have any daughters to talk over their periods with. It was all too gross. Sometimes she pretended her fingers were tickle monsters that would creep under the sheets and grab at the waistband of his boxers.

'What have you got in there, anyway?'

Stephen would scream like a girl and squish himself into the far corner of his top bunk, where his mother couldn't reach him. He had the sheet wrapped tightly around his waist.

'You'll never find out!' Stephen would try to shout and breathe at the same time, laughing. 'This is child abuse!' He would flip back and forth to get away.

'Come on, Stevie wonder. I changed that tush.'

'That was years ago. Things have changed.'

'*Doubt it.*'

Stephen knew it was her way of having the talk without having it. Since his dad was gone. He never told his mother about Ambrose McLean yelling at him. It was his problem and he maintained for ages an awful silence about the smells coming from the house behind Peggy who smiled less and less as she paid Stephen every other week. Finally, she phoned the paper and set up a direct account and Stephen never had to go any more.

Things calmed down. That was his mother, never pushing too hard. His dad used to tickle him until he cried. And then be disgusted and walk away because Stephen was such a wimp.

His mother would still, though he was big, tuck him in and smoothe the sheet. She would rub his back, circumference and radius, circles moving in circles. If he stayed quiet, she would sing, which she almost never did. His dad used to change the radio station if she started singing along. She laughed once in the car and asked him if he didn't like her voice or something.

'Or something,' he said.

But now that he was gone, at nights sometimes she would sing the song she rocked him to sleep with when he was a baby. He heard the tune on his mother's Leon Redbone CD, except Leon called it 'Ain't Misbehavin', and sang different words. It was an okay song, but you couldn't really play the drums to it. Sometimes he imagined hearing it with a reggae beat, or even legato, brushes on snares. Something. He supposed oomph wasn't really the point. He just wanted to coolify it. Make it something a ten-year-old guy could admit liking. Not that he would ever have to admit it. But Stephen could not ever imagine that he would not love that song in the quiet night. It had the effect of making him instantly drowsy and peaceful without tympani, without percussion. The cadence of his mother's voice, her breath going in quiet and coming out only in soft resonance stilled him into sleep.

>*You're just a grubby*
>*Little worm,*
>*I'd like to tickle*
>*You and watch you squirm*
>*I'm misbehavin',*
>*spendin my love on you.*

He bumped the metal lock box at the end of his bed where all his two hundred and seventy-six dollars and forty-three cents were hidden under baseball cards and old Bazooka Joe gum comics. He only turned in his sleep and dreamed of sticks and skins.

Making Tea

AMBROSE WATCHES Connie look with fury under every couch cushion when she loses a pencil. She says, I left it right here, right here on the table and now it's gone. It has my name on it and everything. She asks Peggy and Ambrose again and again, have they seen her pencil. 'No,' Peggy says, 'just get another one from the drawer by the phone.' Connie presses her lips together. Ambrose watches the exchange from behind the paper. How does he know and why doesn't Peggy that it's the losing and not the pencil that is making Connie angry?

You can't make tea until you go down to the kitchen.
  He will not.
  He cannot.
  There should be walls and floors. There should be something to hold on to. There is hunger and dark, a growling hole. He'll end her misery for her.

The Lord has been mindful of us He will bless us. Grammar. Present perfect? Lord has been mindful, continues to be mindful, will be mindful. Will bless us.
  Ambrose is blessed. Except in the most general terms, things he never says out loud. Things he knows and, from long habit, doesn't talk about. Peggy knows they are blessed. Connie knows too. The child of their old age, not quite like Abraham and Sarah. Certainly no concubines involved. Just the usual death, sadness and unexpected rescue. And Alice gone where?
  Ambrose wanted to know what was happening. Ambrose can't think very well. Doesn't know what thinking is. If the brain can be represented as a complex business of circuitry, of electric impulses transferring information easily, swiftly, then Ambrose's brain is

damaged. How would he think? How would he get from A to B? Imagine him at home in a chair that's been his favourite for thirty years. The impress of his backside is proof. No one else fits it or wants to. It's green. It doesn't signify. A sign without a signifier.

This space he occupies. A self and air. Some posture. Some guttural articulation. Labials and sibilants. In place but without sense. Ambrose is in trouble.

What about the chair. It offends him. Someone keeps telling him. He keeps hearing a word. He doesn't like the sound of it. Hearing the word makes his lips pruned with disapproval. Favourite. Consonants. It means Peggy's disgusted. Yes, she is Peggy. She's a she. There's the chair. It's a chair. My favourite.

In his way. In way. Move. Get up. Want some toast. Stomach hurts. Hurts. Hurts. Coffee cup drink coffee. Got to go. Go. Tables chairs sit. Coffee. Black. What?

He lies in bed at night. She sleeps in the other room now. He can't hold his water he can't sleep he can't tell her what's wrong. He can't make these thoughts stick together.

He read about a computer keypad that responds to the slightest touch of a nearly brain-dead carcass and almost formulates necessary thought. Too bad Ambrose won't see that in his time. He has thoughts. Especially when he lies in bed at night. He hears her snore. She goes through what must be like hell in the day, and often in the night. He knows it; he makes it.

He's frightened. There are pictures on the wall. Pictures of him someone he doesn't know. A young girl in a black gown is pinning a flower to his clothing. The woman in the next room tells him it is his daughter Alice on her graduation day. She says to him expectantly, AlicelivesinHalifaxnow. He doesn't know Alice. If he says Alice who, Peggy, it's Peggy and she cries some more. He hates looking at pictures. The eyes are in the wrong place; beneath them, grinning, leering, hungry teeth. See, his wife says, we are all smiling. This is smiling? We were so happy then, she says. You were so proud of

Alice. Ambrose thinks they look hungry. Whoever they are.

Connie comes. He can stay bed think about Connie. She brings the chocolate he can eat. She had to take his padding off one day, soaking. He missed the toilet. No. He didn't take his pants down first. She laughed said, oh Dad, pants are always a pain. Wear a kilt. With the little knife for a pin. You could use it to keep us all away from you when you wanted some peace.

He knows the bed is wet again. She'll find out soon and yell and cry. She'll push him into the other bed and he'll make it wet too. He can go all night. He has to. He's afraid.

The bathroom moves. The climb down, no foothold. He knows it's down. He can't go. Knows she hates him. She says she loves him. She is hard. Her nails hurt his arm when she drags him. Her voice hurts his ears. She gives him orders. She is full of things he has to do, eat, go, speak.

He thinks when he can, sometimes he thinks about the kettle and tea. Bags, not the metal balls or loose leaves. He thinks about making tea. He knows what the kettle looks like. He knows it's not square but round. Ballish. With a wire. No, cord. The points go into the wall. Not on the stove. Not on the gas. The points go into the wall.

He wanted to make tea. Well. It was time. If they gave them tea they would then go home and Peggy and he could clean up and go to bed. He has always liked going to bed with Peggy. He couldn't see where to put water in. The shape was wrong. There was the wire with the points. But it was wrong. He carried it into the living room. Not frightened yet. Peggy turned like a deer will. Saw. He felt warm when she looked at him. He can't seem to make the tea. He didn't say it out loud. He must have spoken. Everyone laughed and Peggy took him into the kitchen and put the square thing away. Then she got the kettle.

Making tea.

You see. He can't help thinking kettle and pot and bag. He can't help thinking that if he'd remembered that time how to make the tea. He'd have been all right. If he'd turned left instead of right, drunk milk instead of coffee, eaten more garlic. Well, Peggy made the tea and used the other thing for hard hot bread. Would you like some toast? she said. And Ambrose yelled when he touched it. So stupid of her not to warn him she'd cooked the bread.

We have it every morning, she said. Well, he thinks he'd know about brown scratchy bread burning his throat every morning. Sometimes he thinks she'll kill him all the while she'll have that puzzled and patient look on her face one day he'll have to slap.

He wanted to boil the water for tea. He doesn't know why she has hidden the boiling thing. There are other ways to make the tea. Yes, she took the kettle before and put it away after the house filled with smoke and the loud noises blared. All the fuss. He was right here.

Ambrose, she said, you've ruined the Russell Hobbes. He doesn't know what she's talking about. If he made her a cup of tea she might cheer up a bit. Cries and cries. He wouldn'a married her if he'd known she was such a sloppy grieter. In Scotland they call it grieting. Havin' a wee griet.

It wasn't always this way, of course. We know that Ambrose has Alzheimer's disease and after he dies we'll find out that it's indeed familial Alzheimer's and after Peggy, his wife dies, but before Alice his daughter does, we'll find out, we the world at large, that the DNA can be manipulated in utero so that the disease becomes marginally treatable. They'll never be able to anticipate simple twists of fate. So much for Alice's tubal ligation. Her baby probably would have been all right. It's ironic, but it's not tragic.

Downtown hockey. Eustace, Ambrose, the hockey game on television. They were too poor to own a television. Some thought it was the devil's instrument. Eustace and he like hockey. They put on scarves, jumpers, gloves, coats, extra socks, so many things done thoughtlessly. He misses that. They walked across the bridge, breathing frost, stand in front of Love's TV, watching six sets of Leafs. They didn't waste words. Eustace brought a thermos of tea once. Pure luxury.

He knows that something is wrong. No one has ever told him what. There are tests, quizzes, endless questions once in a while from a nice young fellow named William who wears a tie and has a good strong voice. He knows how to talk. But never says anything interesting.

'Well, Ambrose, how many coins are on the table?' As if that mattered to anyone.

'Do you know what day it is? Year? Month?' Ambrose doesn't waste his time with idiots.

'Good morning, sir,' he'll say, *'my name's William'* – as if Ambrose didn't know – *'what's yours?'* If you don't know he's not going to tell you.

He goes to the day centre with those poor old souls to brighten them up. He comes home on the big bus after a good day's work.

He has been making tea for sixty years in various countries.

Ways to make tea:

1. gas
2. wood
3. electricity
4. kettles
5. pots
6. a tin can once

He has spent thirty of those years making tea in this house where nothing has changed but for days in a row he doesn't know how to get from the sink to the stove. Today he does. He knows Peggy was crying yesterday. The balled-up tissues are still soggy in the bathroom wastebasket. She's okay today. He can't remember what happened yesterday. He woke from blackness this morning. He doesn't know what's the matter with him but if he had to name it he'd call it fear and robbery. He admired Swiss watches, knew their secrets, maintained their precision with meticulous care. Before the

Japanese bought everything and made it fit for the trash. He made a life with Peggy and Alice. They chose the green carpet – Peggy insists it's taupe – and the dark green furniture. He hung the wallpaper himself. He looked after Connie too when her mum died and she came to be his girl.

But he closed his eyes last night on no memories, no event horizon. His hands shake. Maybe what he's got is a force of gravity so huge that memory is quashed for good. He opened his eyes. In his room is a window with white curtains, a bookshelf, desk, dresser. The usual things. He opened his eyes not knowing. Where is the light? What is light? God? No memory; no prayer. Wait, he said. He can feel his back against the sheet and the mattress. He can feel he is alive. He is something. I.

He wants to write it down. He's scared. How to keep riding his bike and visiting Connie and being with Peg when the scream lives in his throat ready to go.

Connie's lost everyone. Will she guess what it's like to lose knowing? She's his girl. He's old and got a daughter after Alice was gone to university. She seemed delighted with things though she cried for her mother at night behind her bedroom door. The Lord had been mindful of her, blessed her. Now Ambrose thinks, how had the Lord blessed her? With them? He hopes. Life is full of frightening awful things. Connie already knew. She might be angry; she might be frightened. They told her she could trust God. She could trust Him. Because her parents both died? No. Because it wasn't His fault, He didn't blink, was not distracted. Is not distracted.

Connie got married but she's close by and he visits her. He calls her. He takes her to lunch but when it's time to pay she takes his wallet out of his hands and gives the money to the man. This bugs him. Is she stealing his money? No. Is what he says today. But there are leftover thoughts from whatever might have happened yesterday that make him think his own Connie wants the money. She's always had an eye for nice things.

Orange pekoe. Ridgeways on sale at the Bi-Way. What about

Jackson's? She'll never buy Jackson's Earl Grey. Taste is fine. It's all the same, she says. Except she says Earl Grey tastes like dishwater.

'Dishes.'

'Ambrose, I've already done the dishes.'

'Grey.'

'No, sweetie, the dishes are white and green. See?'

'Jack's dishes.' Hot. Listen. Bitey doesn't hear.

'Yes, I'm sure Jack has dishes, whoever Jack is.'

Stupid.

'Amby, where are you going? What do you need? Stop going through the cupboards. You're making a terrible mess.'

'Tea!'

'Here, love. I'll make you some tea. You go through and watch the baseball game. I'll bring your tea in.'

'Dish tea. You'll do it or I'll stand you on your head.'

'Come on, honey, here's your chair.'

'Quit pushing me, stupid.'

'I'm not pushing. I'm just showing you your chair, *Honey*. See? The Blue Jays are playing. Don't You Raise Your Hand To Me, Ambrose. Justyousitdownnow.'

'You're hurting me. Your nails are hurting me. They are so.'

'Ambrose, I cut my nails, see?'

'The dishes.'

'Oh, Ambrose. What about the dishes? I don't know who Jack is or if his dishes are grey. You give me a sore head. Do you want some tea or don't you?'

It should have been clear. She showed him the bruise on her arm this morning and said he gave it to her. Why at this point has she become such a liar? And so stupid.

Tea, well. So many other things. Dr Fortuna says don't drive any more. Anyway, Connie sat beside him in the car like a seeing-eye daughter. You'll want to put your foot on the brakes, now Dad. The light ahead is red. This one's green. Just move your foot to the other pedal.

They made it to the restaurant. He saw Connie shaking. She said, can I drive? I love the way your car goes.

Connie drives a rust bucket. She drove them home.

Home he sits close to her. She's such a youngsweet woman. Warm. She is warm. Plunks beside him on the couch. He wonders. Tongue? She looks at him. He made a mistake. A sweet young mistake. She's warm. Knows she's warm. What else does she know? He's dad, not dad. Old, not old. Tongue, lips. He knows what they're for. Not for Connie. Ambrose, he says to himself though it's an effort, these are not for use with Connie.

With Peggy of the scratchy bitey nails and bossy face.

Peggy's in charge of Ambrose. Drives. Buys him a tie. Steals all his money. He can't buy himself a cup of coffee. She steals his car. Loves him, she cries.

Feeds him rubber stuff. It's pork tenderloin is what she yells at him. Eight ninety-nine a pound. He spits it out on the floor where it belongs. Ambrose, you quit, she says.

I quit.

He likes Dr Fortuna. He speaks up. Tells Ambrose things like he already knows them. Things it seems they have, as men do, most likely already agreed upon. Knows about the bossyface.

How are you?

I'm doing well.

Sleeping?

Yes.

Taking your pills?

Never miss.

Do you worry about what will happen to you?

No.

Is what he says, but he can't pray. He might worry more about this if he wasn't sure that God knows he can't pray, is not startled by his silence, and will engage him in a conversation of considerable length when he's done with this body.

He says to Dr Fortuna, 'I'm fine'. Or sometimes just 'Fine.'

He makes a smile. Vows to be more appropriate with Connie. He doesn't like to make her nervous, but she's warm, happy. He likes that. Maybe Dr Fortuna knows that too.

Things Ambrose can't do:

1. drive
2. kiss Connie that way
3. remember his grandchildren's names
4. make tea

Things Ambrose can do:

1. get his shoes on the right feet
2. sit without falling
3. ride his bike
4. make tea

Peggy finishes his sentences and the sentences of everyone with whom she speaks. Sometimes she does this by guessing the outcome from the clues in the first half. But she has found this to be risky because she's usually wrong or else people quickly modify what they had been intending to say, out of politeness. Peggy is left agreeing with herself. Ambrose knows he has days when he can't finish a sentence because his thoughts seem to stall on a steep hill. Peggy keeps them both company.

His toothbrush. For his teeth. Help, he said he screamed scratchy bitey stolen his tooth ... there it is. The bath is hot, slippery, nope, noway bath. She'll cut him with her nails nope not. Not NOT. Get up. She spends half her life on the floor. Not having a bath don't smell. Look, Peg, I'm ready to go. My belt. Leave it alone. He has underwear on. Plenty. A fella needs his underwear on. Connie doesn't bug scratch bite or yell.

Dad, you stink is what she says she said, but she gave him the washcloth waited while he did it myself. Closed the bathroom door. Peggy left she always leaves Connie stays, laughs, waits, makes coffee. Says, Dad, you don't need six pairs of underwear at once or else your pants won't fit. Doesn't it feel better just to have one?

There is a woman in black with white skin who sits on the end of Peggy's new couch. She stares at Ambrose, frightens him. She looks ferociously hungry, and smells like earth and worms, gap-faced, rotting. Waiting. Ambrose forgets things but when she goes away he doesn't forget her. She is his only memory. Lord, he says and Peggy covers her up with the rug but he can see the outline of her boniness below he knows she hasn't gone away. She is waiting. He goes to the other rooms, he goes to the windows, comes back and she's still there.

There are watch parts in the basement. He sold watch parts to a girl, wheels, gears with scanty jewels. She was going to make earrings out of old watch parts, big market. Ambrose can't fix them now. She gave him thirty-five dollars and he bought coffee for himself downtown where he walked with no jacket. Don't need a jacket. He needed coffee, some coffee, no, some money to get it with. Connie wears watch parts hanging from her ears looks ridiculous and laughing he laughs.

Peggy says let's go to church and they go and then she brings him back to a different house. They didn't go past Muller Brothers' garage on their way home. He didn't see the bears on the high building so he knows that wherever they are this is not home. He's tired, he wants to go home. Get your coat. Peggy says this is home. We're here. See, there's your big old grandfather clock, picture of Connie and Alice. I'll make your coffee and then we'll go to bed. He put his coat back on and found the door but she has stolen the knob and he can't get out. She steals everything, stole his toothbrush, his money, his car keys. I'm calling the police, he says. She picks up the phone and then Connie is there. See, Dad, she says, I'm here to visit you at your house. He says what are you doing here? She says I'm here to visit you at your house. I left my house. I wanted some coffee and a big fat kiss so I came to your house where I know I can get these things so you must take off your coat sit down for some coffee. Let's go home, he says, Peggy. Stupid finally agrees that they are not at home. Connie goes down the hall he hears running water but they're leaving. He says, come on, Connie. She says I'll meet you at your house. Peggy puts the knob back so they can get out. They get in the car and drive home past the two golden bears, the old Wellington building where he had his first watch repair store, up the hill past the hospital to his own front door, which he opens because he knows how to open the door. He smells coffee. There is Connie with cups and cookies, saying, Hi there. He says, what are you doing here, where's Larry and the kids? She says, I just came for coffee. Let's have some, he says, she gives him a kiss.

He can't write any more but he can work the keyboard very slowly. He wants to leave something. Connie says leave yourself and quit leaving me. They are giving him pills that have nothing to do with his diabetes. Peggy says she's not trying to kill him though he's worth more dead than alive. But he's slower.

Pants. Belts. Shirts. Buttons. Laces. Socks. Shoes. How can there be so many things? Pantsbeltshirtbuttonlacessocks shoestoothbrushhairbrushshaver.

Here, Amby, let me help you.

He'll help her.

He'll pants belt her. He'll lace her to something good. He'll do it himself. He knows what he's doing.

He knows how to make the tea. Sauchiehall Street! He knows what he's doing. Ambrose, don't, she says. Ambrose, you'll burn the house down. He'll burn her down old scratchy bitey. He taught Connie how to make tea.

How to make tea:

1. fill the kettle up with fresh, cold water

2. dump the tea from yesterday

3. don't leave the bag in the sink

4. rinse out the pot and fill it with hot water to warm it up

5. dump the hot water

6. put in the new bags and fill the pot with boiling water

7. put on the cosy Peggy likes the tea to scald her lips. Otherwise she's not happy. Put the milk in the cup first. Then pour the tea. Good girl.

Imagine living and breathing and not knowing how to make tea. Larry enjoys many fine cups of tea now and has not once thought to thank me.

Burn. Eyes burn and close. Connie sings sounds. Peggy's tears. Strawberries, cool. Sweet, cool. Connie, spoon, swallow. No tea here. No watches hands gears cleaning solution faces bands. No precision. He utters inanities in response to inanities. How are you what do you do for fun. He sleeps closes his eyes on the burning lack of edges and does not dream he aches.

The Cemeteries Act

SHE SHOULD KNOW about smells because she has her own problem with them. Connie eats apples, one, maybe two a day and leaves the apple cores wherever she happens to be. She likes that I pick them up for her and put them in the composter. But if she's eating one in the bedroom at night, getting the pages of her book sticky, she usually gets rid of the core herself because she hates the smell of rotting apple flesh. She says she'd rather dab the baby's diaper on her wrists or behind her ears.

I can't stand the smell of burning and she knows it. I come home from work and hear her dashing pot lids and when I smell that vile ashtray smell coming from the stove I go back outside into the yard. I know she's come home late from Ambrose and doesn't believe I'd rather make a sandwich or order pizza than smell that smell she's going to call supper.

Connie visits Ambrose two times a week and feels guilty that it isn't four. She goes at all different times because of the kids and going to the university and making supper and she never sees the head nurse, the one in charge of Ambrose, that Peggy is always talking about. This wouldn't be too important except that she has no witnesses. No one to say to Peggy, 'Your beautiful daughter Connie is very devoted to Ambrose, isn't she?' Connie thinks I don't get it but I do. She's scared, she's sure Peggy thinks she never goes. Connie slams doors when I tell her to let Peggy think what she likes. As if it were that easy, she says to me. But she usually makes a good supper when she's mad. Peggy doesn't know she's holding the hoops, so she can't appreciate the way Connie jumps through them. It makes me mad and my garden gets the benefit.

When Connie's really mad she scrubs the children's hands till they're red, cleans the bathroom too. Then she vacuums anything standing still. Joy climbs into my lap whining that it's the only place she's allowed to sit.

'Mom won't let us into the living room.'

'Oh.'

'Why is she like that?'

'Nothing wrong with a clean house.'

'She won't let us sit on the couch.'

'Course not.'

'We can't sit on the couch any more?'

'Nope.'

'Where'll we sit?'

I told her she was condemned to a life sentence on my lap, but she's learned to roll her eyes, just like her mother, because she thinks she's grown up.

Connie says, 'Would you mind if I visit Dad?' Anything less than 'What a wonderful idea' gets me a good supper. Sometimes I'm pretty hungry so I say 'You were just there a couple a days ago. You have papers to mark and the girls have to get ready for camp,' or some such thing. And she stays home. Angry, she makes sauces, gravies, no lumps, salted just right. Last week we had fresh lake trout with a creamy spicy drizzle of something on top, including a parsley garnish and steamed broccoli with cheese sauce. She acts sometimes like she's maybe Joy's age, throwing pots around instead of dolls. If I tell her so her voice gets that sharpness I hate, and she says 'When I was Joy's age I had two more years of having my own mother.' Is this part of the fight or part of the surrender? Her father died when she was six, mother, when she was twelve. Then she went to Ambrose and Peggy. Mostly, she went to Ambrose.

I put orange rind in my nostrils the morning I had to clean the crematorium ducts. Not because of the ductwork but because of the body in the coffin, waiting to be incinerated. They had to shut the furnace down for almost three weeks so I could get in to clean the ash out of the flue. The body had arrived the week after the furnace was turned off. It had a very bad smell that settled in the back of my throat, seemed I had to taste it as well. The orange peels helped for a while.

I had to crawl through thirty yards of ductwork with a vacuum hose, clean out the remains of the remains. No one had lit so much as a lighter in the place for half a month, but the floor and walls and ceiling burned through my knees and shoulders and back. Couldn't stay still. If I had time to think I might have lost my mind in that corridor. Connie asked me how I could stand it. I said I wasn't standing, I was kind of crouched, but she shivered when she should have laughed. There's a ninety-degree angle at the end of the duct where the chimney goes straight up to the sky. I saw dull, particled light dance in the distance; knew I wasn't looking at dust motes. The vacuum hose got wrapped around my chest, tight and hot, hot tuna sandwich smell made me retch. I finished the vacuuming and backed up to the entrance, kicking the tangled hose behind me. Sweating buckets.

Gerald was waiting in the basement when I climbed out. He brought a chair and a glass of icy water. He must have known that anything flavoured, iced tea, lemonade, or single malt Scotch, would taste like the body in the next room. The ice was numbing and I crunched it. I wasn't shaking. He wanted to show me around, wanted to talk. His job was to set the temperature properly for each type of casket, oak or pine or particleboard. After he would sift through the ash with a magnet to pick out the nails and staples. Then he would collect the bones for grinding.

'This useta all be done by hand, ya know. Now it's all electric.'

He showed me the machine for the bones, how he ground them into a fine mulch, then mixed them with the ashes.

'Rose food,' he said, grinning, 'shame ta waste it.'

He turned off the machine. 'See, no splinters. Nothing too obvious. The family appreciates this sorta attention.'

I left for lunch. Tuna sandwich tasted like the smell in the crematorium. I couldn't eat tuna for a long time after that. I couldn't eat my own death and settled for peanut butter.

It was the smell that forced me outside. Connie knows that smell is why I stay outside as much as possible. She says I love the garden more than her. If she gets the mail first she steals the seed catalogues and throws them out. 'You've been digging all day,' she says, 'why do you want to go out there and dig some more? You've got a shovel thing,' she says. 'What's the matter, isn't your penis big enough?' She gets madder when I laugh.

I like her to come with me outside, before the kids figure out I'm home and start with their own long stories. I walk through the ashtray smell of the house. I take her hand and grab the hoe and a cold one and baby the tomatoes and cucumbers sitting patient by the back fence, choking in weeds and dryness. 'I'm not weeding your stupid garden,' she says. She sits down and watches the trail of snail slime.

'Snails,' I say, 'are very bad for my tomatoes.' I crunch the shell under my boot.

'Stupid tomatoes. I hate tomatoes.'

'Don't talk that way. I raised these tomatoes from seed. These are our little baby tomatoes.'

'Seeds,' she says. 'I'm sick of seeds. I hate dirt.'

'I've never asked you to touch a seed, or the dirt. I look after the seeds and the dirt. You go to the mall. That's our deal.'

'Why does everyone love gardening? What's the big deal about growing salad? You don't see people heading to the shed in the morning with a knife to harvest a couple of strips of bacon. What happens to the concept of the grocery store in nice weather? What is the matter with everyone? Even Ambrose grew his own tomatoes, did you know that? Sad, pitiful things they were.'

'Did you see Ambrose today?'

'Yes.'

'You tell him the joke about putting the condoms on with tacks?'

'Yes.'

'I guess he didn't laugh.' I was working between the rows of sweet one hundreds. Connie has an appetite for cherry tomatoes in spite of what she says.

'He wouldn't take his hands away from his face the whole time I was there. I tried to kiss him and hug him. I brought out chocolate. I told him he was an old fart who needed a bath. I told him he stank. If he didn't open his eyes right now I was never coming back. He'd never get another Kit-Kat out of me or a kiss. No more I love you. Niente.'

'And?'

'And he budgeth not.'

I hoped she wouldn't cry until I finished weeding the squash and she didn't. Her voice was very dry and splintered and hurt me the worse. Sometimes I don't get why she puts herself through this. I told her to take me out and shoot me if I ever get like Ambrose. I don't visit him. She passed me the beer without looking up. 'You know I hate the smell of that stuff,' she said. 'Don't come sniffing around me tonight with your face all beery.'

Told her I was thinking how about sniffing right now and she was nice enough to jump up and twine her legs around my middle.

'Just don't kiss me,' she said, sad, angry.

She thinks it's funny I'm good at planting things. She hopes maybe I'll plant Ambrose and he can grow up into a tree she'll sit under, shaded, watering the roots. Connie will be one of those people who visit the cemetery. Aren't many these days. They come for the funerals, leave for the crab canapés and go back to work. They like to stay on the other side of the iron fence. When they drive by they don't look in.

Connie likes to visit me at work. She spends a few minutes watching ants crawl on her parents' monument, sits beside it on the ground, resting her hand on the hot granite edge. Chews a stem of grass, takes in the scenery. Across the road people zip through the McDonald's drive-thru or grab a cone to go from the Dairy Queen. Connie rests. After a bit she gets up and brings me some iced tea and chicken salad from the cooler and we sit on the bench in the sculpture park.

I had her mother's ring reset with a small diamond when she finally said yes, she'd marry me. I knew she liked me for a long time and I knew it bugged her that she liked me. No degrees, no tie. I drove a motorcycle in those days. She couldn't resist my charm I guess. Connie wears that ring with her wedding band, or sometimes by itself. She likes a lot of her mother's things around her. Wears her mother's old clothes or puts the vegetables on the table in the serving bowls that had been hers. Now she's started wearing Ambrose's old undershirt.

I like the crunch of the shovel when it cuts through sod. Rolling back the grass, I tell her it's like peeling off her stockings. 'Show me.' She shivers when she says this. She asked me once if I thought her legs looked like frog's legs and wouldn't speak to me for days when I said yes.

She's naked. Jumps off the bed to pull on her long black stay-ups. The ones she bought the night of Stella's party. That night she rang the doorbell, heard the footsteps coming and quick as a flash, lifted her skirt to show me where the lace met her thigh before turning to give Domenic a smack on the lips. She does things like this with no discussion, ever, as if maybe she sneaked such behaviour past herself.

She wants me to bury Ambrose. Crying sometimes, says she hopes it's soon. A man on Ambrose's floor is in the hospital now. Rushed across the street in an ambulance. Pneumonia. He might not last. 'The doctor,' she says, 'the doctor turns to the wife and kids, two young banker types, and asks,' Connie says, *'he asks with utmost delicacy*, "How aggressive would you prefer the treatment to be?"' Then she starts talking about the Dutch supposedly carrying around anti-euthanasia cards that say please don't kill me. Please try to save my life.

The guy's family, they're new to this, they want aggressive treatment, they want to save the old guy's mindless life. I see she thinks about that poor old guy in the hospital; wonders what she'd answer. I know what I'd say. Death couldn't be worse.

Ambrose shuffles along. Even though he's diabetic she takes him chocolate when she goes. He's too thin, she says. You should see the food up there. Absolutely full of nutrition, she says. So laden with nutrition, Ambrose can't lift the fork to his lips, it's such organic crap.

I never told her I went to see him once by myself. I went only a couple times before, always with her. What if he's the future? is what I think. I'd rather put my head in the sand than face that. But he was a man once who'd look you in the eye when he talked, and tell you straight. You can't ignore that.

Last Thursday I was supposed to exhume a body. So I start but then the cops come and lawyers and yelling families and papers waving grey suits everywhere. So then they say, come back in an hour. The cemetery isn't far from the Health Centre and Ambrose looked happy to see me. Like he knew he should know me. He was walking along so I did too, took his arm, told him it was a hot one. Some of the men were in tie-back gowns showing diapered backsides. Do I hope I die before this happens to me? Do fish swim?

He's her father. He still looks pretty good. Too thin, white and cold as though he'll be heading my way soon. Shakes hands though. Likes to try out a wink and a nod. Like we're just laughing at a joke but I don't know who it's on.

He had words with me only once. About Connie before she married me. He said I wasn't making her happy, wasn't treating her nice. If I didn't shape up he'd put a stop to things. He wasn't kidding around. No smiling, no conversation. I shaped up.

We went to the dining room. It's nice. Windows, flowers. There's a piano nobody plays and a juice bar but they have to ask for a cup. They can't get it for themselves. A guy in the corner, named Frederick, was looking at TV. When an old girl with no teeth came in I thought she was walking in circles like a half dozen others but she stopped at old Fred there, who didn't know it was his lucky day, and straddled his leg. Started rubbing herself back and forth, dead quiet and halfway furious. Fred stared straight ahead at good old Alex Trebek. I laughed watching Alex keep on doing Jeopardy while she kept on doing Fred. Who was crazier? I would have felt better if at least one of them seemed to be having fun. Nurses came in and put a stop to things. Ambrose looked like he got the joke.

I do the landscaping, supervise the perpetual care, make sure the pathways are graded nice. Things haven't changed much at work in a couple hundred years; there's some comfort in that. I stay away from the perimeter on the Woolwich Street side. I don't like to look up from the old pitted limestone markers to see Ronald McDonald leering at me, knowing I'll join this solemn congregation while he lives on. Good neighbour, though. Employees cross the street every day to pick up the greasy wrappers that collect along the fence.

I like the iron fence, though *Park and Cemetery* says people would hang around more without it. Would my daughter really like to have her wedding pictures taken here? Or go jogging along these quiet paths? The guy writes, why not stock the ponds with trout and open the chapel for weddings? *Death is a part of life*. The guy who wants to make the cemetery a 'viable community resource' open for 'passive recreation' hasn't yet yelled at his mother for taking her last breath or looked at his daughter in that way Connie has. Where I see she's wondering, should I start writing things down for her in case I die next month and she won't know what I'm like or how I love her?

I like the iron fence. It made me smile the day I started work here. Founding fathers built it to comply with Ontario statutes that still say a fence has to be around cemeteries to keep wandering cattle out. Just see those cows going straight from coffee and doughnuts at Tim Horton's to the succulent Kentucky bluegrass at the Woodlawn Big C.

Of course the fence keeps out vandals, young kids prove they're invincible by knocking down a few old headstones. Lovers try to sneak in for an extra thrill. One night I stepped out from behind a bush in front of two such. Girl froze, young hero staggered back, fell flat on his ass, cursing and scrambling to get back over the fence while I offered my arm to his girlfriend and walked her out. She was laughing. It's a serious fence, spiked, dignified. You cross it, you go somewhere else. Connie says 'a place of clearly defined expectations'. Gives privacy to think or pray or relax because the cemetery mower blades set at one and a half inches above the ground and won't dwarf the root system.

Connie likes me to recite the Cemeteries Act in bed. She knows it's my job to 'ensure that quiet and good order are maintained in the cemetery at all times', and so when she's at me, says between breaths, don't forget, quiet...and...good order ... must ... be ... maintained ... and I say I'm not in the cemetery and she says I'll soon have you there....

We don't own any property. The term is 'property' now. Was 'plot'. Before that, 'grave'. Cutting-edge jargon in the front office they might offer you an initial price on 'interment rights' and when they see you don't get it they scale down to plot.

She wants me to do the grave for Ambrose. A nice enough grave can be done in about a half hour, but she knows I'll take my time with the backhoe and the finishing. I'll be glad it's over. I'll shine up the lowering device and cover the earth with flowers and clean turf. Make sure the edges are cribbed. 'Ambrose likes everything nice,' she says. 'When he goes six feet under it's to be done properly.' I know she's done some thinking about it. She wants to have it right in her mind.

'Now it's only about five feet under,' I say.

'Five feet?'

'Yep. R.S.O. Body must be covered by at least two feet of dirt.'

'Why two? Why not three? Why not one?'

'Three's too much. One's not enough. Got to be two.'

'You're sure?'

'I'm sure.'

'Okay. And no concrete liner, right?'

'No liner.'

'Ambrose will be biodegradable,' she says, as though having him in the earth settles something for her. Though she knows Ambrose was always sure about heaven, quoting his Bible about *mysterious changes* and *corruptible bodies becoming incorruptible*. Even now, in the Health Centre, when I asked while we were walking the hall, 'Ambrose are you going to heaven?' He met my eye and said, 'You better believe it.'

Our neighbour, Domenic, understands about cemeteries. Even

seems to understand Connie's need to be exact about Ambrose. He believes in life after death, pays his respects to his dead mother once monthly. Stella and Domenic bring the kids to visit Nonna. Domenic's only fear of the cemetery is the beer store beside it, the chance he'll be mugged by some guy desperate for a case of Fifty. He brings the kids and then they all go to the park for a Shopsy's all-beef dog with plenty of mustard. He and Stella bought interment rights. They stop by on the way out to visit their *bungalow*. 'This is where we retire, eh, Larry?' he says. Stella says, 'We woulda bought for the kids but they'll probably get married and move away.' Meanwhile their Robert is still in Pampers. Stella and Domenic take the long view.

I don't take the long view. Connie calls me the daily guy. Go to work daily, play with the kids, fix the everlasting drip in the bathroom faucet, work on growing my own salad. I know I'm above the ground for a while, working the hoe, laying mulch and planting tulip bulbs for those bodies at rest or in hell or finished or redeemed. I don't know for sure. I wish I did.

When I climb the stairs to bed at night, I can feel my back is sunburned. Sometimes I still have soil under my fingernails; this makes Connie either kick me out of the bed or pull me in fast. Later, it's quiet, I think how I like my job in the big field across from the fast food strip.

It's a big thing, watching Ambrose die. I try not to think about it. I wish Connie could take a vacation from thinking about it. I know she'll come to visit where Ambrose is buried, where he plain isn't. I've been cutting off the stalks of ripening flowers, tying a paper bag over the seed heads so that when they split, the seeds will fall into the bag. I'm making my own seed packets so Connie can plant some bee balm and foxglove around the headstone. I've made a good supply of compost, just from her bad apple habits. She'll have an outfit for planting, too, a white T-shirt and a short skirt that with luck will slide up when she bends. I'll drop the shovel and sneak a peek and Connie will laugh as she plants. She'll put in some of those stargazer lilies she makes me buy for her at eight bucks a pop. She'll want a holly bush, a dwarf one, so there will be green at Christmas. She will rake the soil there, turning it over, watching out for the worms while she is running it through her fingers, making it pliant and bare. She will smooth the earth, working up a sweat, grieving over crabgrass and dandelions, and wresting them out. Dirt or no dirt, she loves these flowers. She will guard them against theft and blight. She will tend them, she will fuss and prune and water them, tending them as she tended him.

Mitigations

GORD USES HIS TONGUE to push the damn tooth out. There goes another one. A bicuspid. He still has his molars and, he hopes, nice breath for a man with such bad teeth. Well, not actually bad teeth.

'It's your gums, Gord,' is what the dentist had said. 'You need a periodontist. I can set you up with an appointment probably as early as September.'

'No kidding.' Which sounded like 'Nahh ka-ahn.' The suction hose kept sticking to his tongue. That was in April. Late April. If he made the appointment right then the specialist would be prepared to consult with him in four months about slicing open all of his gums and packing bondo in so he could keep the rest of his teeth. Gord swished the silver grit out of his mouth with a fluoride rinse. Vileness upon vileness. Insult to injury. Spitting into the vacuum with a frozen mouth. Fluoride, drool, silver dropping onto his jeans. He wanted to get back to work. He wanted to run the revs on his bike. He wanted to take off the bib.

The tooth looks good. Not a mark on it. He puts it under his pillow and pulls on his jeans. No blood. That's what scares him. Like his whole mouth is dead under the skin.

He drives his Harley to work, feeling the thrub of the engine. Is it making his teeth rattle?

Gord lives in jeans and T-shirts. He has boxes of Nikes in his closet for work. If he goes anywhere else he wears boots. His mother bought him sandals last year for his birthday. Tevas, expensive leather ones, with Velcro. He can't wear them. He leaves them by the door in case his mother comes to visit. Turns one upside down so it looks like he's just kicked them off on his way in with a bag of groceries. When they were new he dragged them around behind his bike on a gravel road. Wore them in the shower so they'd take the impress of his foot. He loves his mother. Dolores is a noticing kind of a woman. He knows how she thinks: Tevas are cool. If he wears them then he will be cool and maybe she'll get a daughter-in-law and perhaps a granddaughter. She would have given it thought. He would like to live up to her expectations. It's not that he's shy about his toes. It's the Velcro. The sound of it.

Gord lives at the back of an old red brick house on a shaded street in what used to be known as the Italian section. There are apartments, one upstairs, one down, and Gord's place, a clapboard addition stuck on the back of the house. The grey paint chips off whenever he closes the door. It matches the grey on the slanting carport where the two families renting the house proper park their cars. It leans now to the left because Angela, the downstairs wife, backed into the centre beam with her Plymouth Fury. She was in a hurry. Angela often rushes past Gord, supporting her baby on one hip, using her jangling car keys as an inadequate counterbalance. The weight of responsibility keeping her upright. She takes the baby to play group, although Gord thinks it is too young to play. 'I'm off to play group, Gord,' is what she announces if he is outside working on the bike. Or, 'I'm going to get groceries Gord, do you need anything?' Or, 'Evan's got another ear infection. Can you believe it?' It's surprising to Gord that she doesn't hit more things. Angela runs to the doctor's, scoots over to the pharmacy, zips out for lunch, jingling the keys and bouncing the baby in the direction of her enormous car. Past Gord who applies firm pressure to the ratchet, satisfied with the hasping catch of it.

Gord doesn't use the carport. In the summer the bike stays outside under a canvas-and-wood shelter he built and in the winter he heaves it up a makeshift ramp through the door of his apartment into the living room. He keeps a slab of hard maple on the floor so the kickstand won't dent it. He empties the gas tank and covers the bike with a thick flannel sheet until the weather turns.

He wants to get back to work. His photo ID has a bar code that lets him into the secure floor. He waits on the other side of the tempered glass door until the coast is clear. Then he swipes the card and slips in before any of the patients can get too close to the door and maybe get out. Not that he couldn't muscle them back in, or coax, or even suggest. Most of his patients are passive. Most of them are old. It's Grace, usually, who sits by the door with her purse and her suitcase. A fine Burberry's trench draped neatly across the chair beside her. When Gord walks by she says politely, 'Excuse me, young man. Do you know what time my son will be here? I haven't got all day.'

Gord smiles. All day is what Grace has. All day every day.

'Now, Grace, I don't know. Why don't you come into the lounge and I'll make you some tea. You'll be able to see the door if your son comes in.'

'Well. I wouldn't want to miss him. I can't understand what's taking him so long. I want to go home.'

Gord lifts her coat and suitcase with one hand and offers Grace his arm. 'Just you come and have a comfortable chair here, Grace, and I'll put the kettle on.'

Grace stands. 'I guess it'll be all right. I'll just tell this girl to watch for Francis.' She approaches the nurses' station as if it's the front desk of the Royal York. Gord watches. She looks for the bell on the counter. Finds it and hits it. Alison comes out from the office.

'Yes, Grace?'

'If my son Francis comes – I'm expecting him any moment– could you please have him meet me in the lounge?' Alison looks at Gord. She's new to the floor. Alison says yes of course, not knowing she's dismissed as soon the request is made. Not knowing that Grace's son hasn't visited for months. Gord knows. He takes Grace's elbow, escorts her to a wing chair, and brews some English Breakfast.

'Gordon, I want to go home now. Call my son, please.'

'I know, Grace. We'd like you to stay with us a while longer. Don't you like it here? Are you uncomfortable?'

Grace puts the saucer on the table. It scrapes across the melamine. Her hand is at her collar again, twisting. 'Call my son, please.'

'Grace, it's just not time to go home yet.'

'Call my son, Gordon. Call Francis. He can't have meant to leave me here.' Her voice is getting louder.

'I'm sorry, Grace.' Gord doesn't want to lie. He doesn't want to say, yes, and then not do it. Some patients would forget. About going home Grace never forgets.

She turns on him. *I want to go home, you bastard!'*

'I know, Grace.' Gord is used to being a bastard. He pours Grace some tea and sits with her. Offers her a biscuit. He pulls a Kleenex from the box on the table and puts it in Grace's hand. She presses it to the corners of her eyes and to her nose before tucking it into her sleeve. Gord looks away. Ambrose, he notices, is sitting in the sun near the window. He sits with his elbows on the arms of the chair, head down. Watching his feet. Peggy has been to see him today with fresh shirts and trousers. Gord admires Peggy's devotion to starch and steam. If a dose a day were the cure for Alzheimer's, Ambrose would have been home months ago.

Gord looks after Ambrose too. Helps him keep clean and fed. Ambrose doesn't know that what he's doing is relying. For months he would come to the Health Centre in the afternoons, three days a week, so Peggy could have a break from looking after him. In the early days he would tell her he was going to visit his brother Sam, now seated in the wheelchair next to Ambrose by the sunny window. 'Well, Peg.' He would put on his fedora. 'I'm off to visit those poor old souls.' When the Out and About bus dropped him at the Centre, Gord was the one waiting for him by the door.

'Hello, Ambrose.'

'Hello there, Mr Lawrence.'

'Aw, Ambrose. Come on now, call me Gord.'

Ambrose would salute and the two men would go in. Gord and Peggy and the staff encouraged the myth that Ambrose was some kind of volunteer for the local Alzheimer's chapter. He knew about the disease. His sisters had both died incoherent and emaciated, having forgotten the use of words and food. He was active at first, going bowling, helping with woodworking projects. They would test him sometimes. See how far things had progressed. Regressed.

When he couldn't tell the circle among the squares any more he got surly. Gord would say, 'Ambrose, what doesn't belong here? Something's different from the other things. What is it?'

Ambrose would stare for a while at the table. He'd clean his nails and push his chair away. 'Dumb thing,' he'd say and he would look at the wall, study the pattern in the paper hung there.

Gord wonders at his own inclinations. Why work here? Why witness and aid this lengthy apprenticeship to death? He's a good nurse. He has money. He could stay in a good hotel between periodontal appointments and order room service. Take a year off to coax his teeth back to health. He could get on his bike and ride through rain and ice to better weather. He loves his Harley. He maintains it with care. It keeps people at a distance. They see his hair, jacket, black bike and they make room when he merges with traffic. He likes being part of the landscape, but knows he's also taking his life in his hands. He's seen other bikes, Suzukis, Hondas, even BMWs get badly cut off. Gord has watched these guys kick down the stand at a traffic light and slam their boot into the doors of Camrys driven by old ladies who never even saw the guy they just about killed. Gord knows he is not known. Knows he is seen and kept clear of.

Clocks were the worst. Ambrose had been a watchmaker for forty-seven years in the town where he was born. Clocks he knew intimately. He had fine hands, steady and clean, handling small gears and jewels with elegance. Gord showed him pictures of clocks. What time is it now, Ambrose? What time is it now? It was quarter to six. It was nine-thirty. It was noon. How do you know it's noon and not midnight? Because the sun's face is showing behind the numbers. You can see it. Gord had not noticed this himself. One day the hands were all pointing down and to the left. In every picture. This is what happens to people with Alzheimer's disease even if they have built clocks from scratch. Gord knows. Eventually all the hands point down and away. They cluster, as though for comfort.

Ambrose knew clocks. Why was Gord so daft? Such a decent fella. Showing him the same picture over and over again. He walked away from the table and headed for the door. He was going home.

Gord's impressed by the number of patients who want to go home. They head for the door like it's the start of the brightly lit tunnel. The door through the iron curtain. Out of this nonsense. Home is not where the heart is. Gord knows it's the place where fists fly, where Grace used to like to suck mothballs, believing they were Tums and would settle her stomach. Where, if Peggy slips out to the bank, Ambrose forgets bread in the toaster and the neighbours call the fire department and the whole place reeks of burning. Gord knows the trouble these guys cause.

In the Health Centre Ambrose doesn't cause trouble. Not for Gord. Seventy years of being a tidy, modest man have left Ambrose fundamentally defined, Gord thinks. The definition has settled in the joints and muscles of Ambrose's body, which seems to act by rote in spite of the brain's atrophy. Put a toothbrush in Ambrose's hand and he'll brush his teeth. Pass him the comb. He might look at it, wondering, but if Gord moves Ambrose's hand toward his head, the comb is lifted and Ambrose will organize his fine, damp hair as he always has. Between them, Gord and Peggy keep Ambrose clean. Peggy does all his laundry. He might have to wear grey elasticized trousers from Zeller's, but Peggy will iron sharp creases into the legs, the way she did when her husband was a busy man, taking the stairs to his shop two at a time. Though Ambrose, in his runners with the broad Velcro strap across the instep, merely shuffles now.

Gord stays beside Ambrose when he walks. Falling, he knows, is the worst thing and also the most likely. Gord's patients don't move much. The blood doesn't move in old veins, which seem themselves to be as dry and brittle as archaic bones. There seems little that is vital.

He takes slow steps with Ambrose, guarding, making conversation.

'Lookin' good today, Ambrose.'

'Today and every day.'

'Jays are doing well. I think they might take the series. Watch the wheelchair there, Ambrose.'

'You watch it.'

'Don't worry, buddy. I'm watchin' it.'

He plans long trips. Sometimes he takes all of his holidays at once. Grace and Ambrose and Ken and Lucia he puts out of his mind. Last year he rode to California, around the great lakes, across the Midwest and down and over, liking the bike's will, as it always seems to him, to stay upright. The balance and motion make him feel that he is in the company of something good.

It was a good trip and a bad trip. The good parts he can't really remember. All through Ontario the engine didn't fail, the rain didn't come. It wasn't cold. He accomplished the distance easily, holding his wrist steady on the throttle and ignoring the numbness in his ass. Gord drove north out of California, up through Idaho and into the mountains in Wyoming where the weather suddenly changed. At first the rain felt good, cooling him off, soaking his leather gloves so that he could feel his fingers inside wrinkle and prune. But with the altitude, the rain changed to slush and finally to snow. Gord took off his sodden gloves and pulled empty bread bags out of his pack to wrap around his raw hands. He kept thinking, *If I just keep driving I will drive right out of this.* Gord concentrated on the weather and the road. He heard the exhaust pipe rattling, loosened by the vibrations. When the engine began to miss he pulled over. He was on his knees in the snow beside the Harley with a T-shirt he used to dry off the points. He started on the exhaust bolt, but his hands were too cold, too numb to hold on as he turned the ratchet. When they slipped, he scraped his knuckles on the frame. He watched it happen, watched the blood rise quickly and drop onto the snow, but couldn't feel it right away. Wouldn't feel it for another hour. He was driving, looking for the other side of the storm. He saw the eighteen-wheeler up the road skate sideways with some grace into the ditch. His clothes were frozen to his skin and his hands were red. There were breadcrumbs in the cracks where the skin had been cut. *Raindrops keep*

falling on my head, but that doesn't mean my eyes will soon be turnin' red.
If he kept driving he would be all right. He kept one hand pressed
between his thigh and the engine, one hand on the throttle. His
stubble was thickly frosted. Just on the other side of Wampsutter the
highway patrol closed the road. Impassable. *No kidding*, he says. He
turned the bike around and skidded back into town. There were no
hotel rooms left so Gord went to a bar and started drinking coffee.
He looked up when a guy in full leathers sat down beside him.

'Nice day for a ride.'

'Beautiful.'

'Where you from?'

'Canada.'

'You must feel right at home. You get a room?'

'No, but I'm planning to carve an igloo in that park over there.'

'No shit, man.'

'No.'

'That your Harley?'

Gord turned. A question like that in the middle of nowhere could
be trouble. Harleys make guys want to fight for some reason. He
thought he could probably take him.

'Yes.'

'Cool.'

'Pretty damn cold.'

'No shit, man.' The guy's shoulders started to shake. The snot at
the end of his nose wobbled and Gord looked at him and saw what
he thought was probably a mirror image of himself. He started to
laugh. Each of them, soaked to the skin, hair greased up like a punk
accident, and raw, red hands wrapped around mugs of coffee.
Laughing now uncontrollably. Mike said, 'I g-guess if w-we're not
g-gonna freeze to d-d-death we might as well die laughin.' Gord
kept trying to stop, taking deep breaths and not looking at his new
best friend. He would get control, hear Mike snort beside him, and
be off again, tears streaming, gut aching. They moved to a table to
eat burgers. Mike said he had a room Gord could share if he felt like
it.

'Figure you might need a place. You know it when you're out travelling alone, specially on that bike, the dogs bark at you, kids stare at you, and nobody talks to you.' Gord accepted the offer. He didn't ask Mike's last name. Never saw him after. In the morning he sat in a T-shirt and underwear at the laundromat, reading the paper and waiting for his clothes to dry. Moving his tongue gently around against the smooth insides of his teeth. The roads were clear and Gord headed for home though it pained him to keep the throttle opened with his hand sometimes bleeding.

Gord takes a long weekend to get his bike ready for the Maritime trip at the end of the month. Tuesday morning Ambrose falls. Badly. Gord is with him, walking the corridor, making conversation. He doesn't like to look in Ambrose's eyes, which have, in the merest three-day absence, become suddenly vacant. He keeps his mind on the moment, watching out for Ambrose's safety, thinking about what he has to do next, who needs pills, who needs a diaper change. He turns for a second, the time it takes to swivel your head on your neck first in one direction and then back, say west, and then east and done. Ambrose is on the floor. Flat, face first, moaning. Gord sees him go down like a tree. Can't get the A in Ambrose out. Stutters like his mouth is full of Novocaine. Ambrose is on the floor moaning. Ambrose is on the floor moaning and bleeding, forehead, nose, chin, all in contact with the hard cold floor. Gord yells for Alison and Beth who come alongside. He feels down Ambrose's back and legs and gently turns him onto his side. There is blood on his face and shirt, dripping onto Gord's arm. Ambrose has closed his eyes. Red bubbles at his nostrils inflate and burst and Gord is delighted to see them. Ambrose is breathing. They are all breathing.

'Ambrose.' Gord prays the name. Invokes it. Needs the last thirty seconds back. 'Alison, get a gurney. Call Dr Martin or get whoever's on call up here. Ambrose, can you hear me? Can you open your eyes?'

Ambrose's eyes are already swollen. His nose is twisted to the left. Blood runs from his lips. Gord forces a finger into Ambrose's mouth. The tongue is there. No obstruction. But there are bits of teeth which Gord tries to remove.

'You need gloves.'

'Get me some then.' Ambrose's blood is on Gord's hand. There are scabbed cuts on Gord's hands from fixing the Harley. If Ambrose has AIDS, so does Gord now. Stupid. But he had to make sure. He keeps his hand over Ambrose's heart. It's beating steadily. Two more orderlies come and the four of them together make a crib for Ambrose with their arms and lift him to the gurney. Gord holds him on his side to keep the blood from going down his throat. The blood is on the floor. And it's on Ambrose's plaid shirt and pressed trousers and on Gord's shirt and on the stretcher sheet. Ambrose keeps his eyelids closed. They are vermilion now.

Gord's landlord, Elmer, does not mind the bike in the house. If he notices it's there. Elmer sometimes stops by to say hello and to ask again if Gord wouldn't like to buy the house. Elmer wears green work pants, the kind plumbers like. They hang down his bum in the regular way in spite of the thick red suspenders he uses for support. Elmer wants to sell the houses he owns around town. He's been landlording so generously and for so long that his spine is bent with the weight of his responsibilities. He can't square his shoulders. He can't straighten up and fly right. He wants to watch TV or go to Florida like other people his age. He doesn't want to have to fix things that he owns, but that other people break and then complain about.

'You know those people upstairs.'

Gord knows. Trish and Rocky. Well, Trish calls him Rocky. *Rocky honey.* But Gord knows that Rocky's friends, friends who say, 'Come on, punch my gut, come on, hard as you can, I dare ya,' call him Rock. Gord doesn't call him anything.

'They took a knife to the freezer. Called and said, "Elmer, there's somethin' wrong with this fridge. No, we don't know what happened." ' Elmer exaggerated his vowels and pinched his voice, doing a pretty good impression of Trish.

'I know what happened. They took a knife to the gal-darned refrigerator. And. You know what they got sitting in the can up there? What *Rocky honey's* keeping maybe a little too close to the toilet? Oxy-acetylene tanks!'

'Tanks?'

'Tanks.'

'Like, for welding?'

Elmer gives the sharp downward stroke of a nod, but can't, or won't raise his head yet.

'For welding,' he says to the floor. 'Now, what happens if he farts? What happens if he cuts the blue cheese? He looks the kind that lets go some good ones. I think we're lookin' at nuclear holocaust, Gordon. I think you better be digging yourself a bomb shelter back there. Tell me this, anyway. What's Rocky gonna do with his welding tanks up in the bathroom? What's he need 'em there for?' Elmer looks up. 'His little metal prick fall off?'

'Elmer.' Gord is laughing. Not only to be having this conversation, but to be having it with Elmer whose hearing aid is so old and is turned up so loud it's clicking and giving feedback, echoing the words as Elmer speaks.

'Had to be a whole new gal-darned fridge.'

'Frost-free?'

'Do I look stupid?'

Elmer's eyebrows climb up toward his scalp when he asks this question. They're visible above the thick glasses he wears whose plastic frames are held together in the centre with masking tape. The two sides adhere, but the match is bad, askew, as though Elmer joined two halves of odd glasses to make a whole. Elmer lights another cigarette, leaning against the kitchen counter. His stoop makes it difficult for him to sit down so he stands to tell Gord again about the proposed terms of sale. He butts the ashes into his hand. He talks and butts until his hand is full. Gord moves to get a saucer for Elmer, but when he turns around he sees Elmer's ash hand withdrawing, empty, from his pocket. Gord thinks about Elmer's hardworking wife, going through her husband's pockets for loose screws, ragged Kleenex, mint-flavoured toothpicks before doing the laundry. Elmer offers to take back the mortgage and to keep the deal a secret from the tenants. They could be informed of the imminent sale, evicted, and then Gord could rent to whomever he chooses and *damn the freezer-pickin' whiners to heck.*

'To heck?'

'You heard me. I don't mince words.' Again the vigorous down-stroke. Elmer's eyes are cast down. His arms folded across his chest, which mutes the whine from the hearing aid's amplifier that's clipped there. The cigarette butt is gone. Gord assumes it's in Elmer's pocket.

'It's a good offer, Elmer. I appreciate it. You should sell and you should go to Florida. I don't see you a relaxing kind of a guy, though. Might drive you crazy. You might end up with me looking after you.'

The suggestion of senility makes Elmer laugh. The hearing aid echoes the wheeze in his lungs. 'Well, now. You might be right about that. But the wife's had enough. Wants me home more. She wants to go out for dinner. Can you imagine me sitting still at a restaurant? Letting some light-in-the-loafers waiter put a napkin in my lap? How'd I get the ashes where they go? Probably wouldn't let a man smoke a decent cigarette. Forget Florida, Gord. That there's enough to drive me to the loony bin and don't spare the horses.'

Gord knows little enough about what drives his patients to his own part of the loony bin. He only knows what to do with them once they get there. Ambrose went over like a felled tree. He forgot to put his hands out. He probably forgot that he had hands, or that people who are perpendicular to the floor and who are suddenly, rapidly about to smash their faces into it need to perform some act of mitigation. Gord could not move fast enough. At night in dreams he wakes up slowly and hot, turning his head west and then east to see Ambrose fall. He falls a dozen times without hitting and Gord is ready. He's ready to catch Ambrose. He knows what's coming. In dreams he can splice that moment into constituent parts with so much time to insert himself and change the outcome. Sometimes he puts his arms out. In the dream sometimes Gord rescues him. Sometimes he pulls his arms away at the last minute. As though he's Bugs Bunny working with the fat trapeze artist. Sometimes it's his mother who falls. Sometimes he pushes her. Gord has moved the TV into his room since Ambrose fell and he keeps the remote control near his bed.

Since he fell Ambrose has been eating puréed meat and Jell-o. When that started to choke him he had to have his diet supplemented with Ensure. Good name, Gord thinks. It ensures enough calories for survival. A meal in itself. Ambrose has a hard time remembering to swallow. The technique has been short-circuited by knots and tangles in the brain. Ambrose is a head case. Gord is used to sitting beside him quietly with the tall glass of thick liquid and a straw, urging Ambrose at intervals to take sips. Ambrose tries to comply. His eyebrow is stitched. It's ugly and no mistake about it. His eyelids and cheekbones are every shade of green and purple and yellow. The swelling in his nose has subsided, but teeth are missing. There are black gaps in his smile and dried blood on his gums that either never goes away, or that gets renewed, like stigmata. Sometimes when Peggy comes Ambrose smiles. Not often but sometimes. And Peggy bursts into tears. She is the only woman Gord has ever seen about whom this is true. Peggy comes into the common room, smiling and courteous to the patients and staff. If Ambrose should look up and smile, Peggy's face turns red and tears spring from her eyes before she can get her hanky out. Gord can hear her scolding herself. 'Come on now, Peggy. Come on. Come on.' It seems to work. By the time she crosses the room she's under control and ready to approach Ambrose's battered face with a kiss. A kiss he usually rejects.

Sometimes Gord worries about his own smile. He hasn't lost a tooth since April, but he also hasn't seen the periodontist. He flosses and brushes and uses his gum stimulator religiously. But he knows he has the teeth of an old man. He thinks about trying a bit of the Ensure. The label reads, 'Nutritious and tasty.' He's looking forward to another bike trip, he's never been down east. Maybe he should go to Florida, tell Elmer he's going to scout it out for him. He hopes the house doesn't sell for a long time. He'll never get another landlord who pays for cable.

He stretches the stiffness out of his neck. Peggy has the glass of Ensure for Ambrose, but it doesn't look as if he wants any more. Any more of anything. When Gord gets him ready for bed that night he notices the swelling of Ambrose's abdomen. Thinks maybe it's not too bad, maybe he just didn't see before how skinny Ambrose's legs are. But there's something starved about Ambrose, like something is eating him alive. It's not just the Alzheimer's and Gord knows that the truth of this is both bad and good. He feels with his tongue along his gum, thinking. Ambrose breathes out when Gord lays him back on the pillows and the breathing sounds like a moan. The kind of sound you maybe only thought you heard.

The One with the News

AMBROSE CAME BACK from the dead last night. Worm-eaten, stinking of compost gone awry. He was happy to see me and to be back and in his right mind with Peggy. She kept picking up grey bits of flesh from the carpet, shaking her head at his untidiness, yet delighted nevertheless to have him home. I knew that days were passing in my dream, and as they did, he began to look better. The flesh adhered more specifically to his face; I couldn't see so much of his gums when he smiled. He seemed to grow lips during dinner. At the soup course, I distinctly heard his teeth clacking together, but by the time he was eating the hazelnut torte, I could hear smacking noises. I also knew that he got better because I was there.

This dream made me wish I had a therapist. I told Larry about it in the morning and I asked him if he'd ever seen a body coming out of a grave instead of going into one. He supervises the burial crew at Woodlawn but he's also in charge of exhumations. He gave me a kiss and said 'Forget it, Connie, you're scary enough.' He didn't want to give me any details. I didn't need them.

I have a scar on my knee from falling on the sidewalk in front of Wendy's house when we were six years old. We played what time is it Mr Wolf and I turned, screaming, to run away from Kevin McPhee who was the wolf. I tripped on the same heaved up concrete that made me fall off my bike the week before. I had just lost the scab and there I was, bleeding and crying. The object of my friend's disgust. I don't remember Wendy ever falling. My father heard me and came to take me home. He put another Band-Aid on my knee and read to me about Nubbins the farm horse, who had a pretty good life.

This was before my father died. I remember the press of the cold kitchen table against my thighs. It seemed strange and thrilling that it was my father peeling back the Band-Aid and gently pressing it to my skin, and not my mother. I didn't know he would be able to do such a thing at all, let alone with great gentleness. He didn't live much longer after that. As though God decided that this one act should be enough to last me until Ambrose came along.

When I was ten years old my mother bought a three-bedroom cottage on the Deer River in the Kawarthas. I think it was the Kawarthas. I used to listen to the weather reports for Haliburton, Muskoka, and the Kawarthas. Which are we, I asked my brother. He was fishing and didn't care.

The cottage stood three feet off the ground on concrete blocks. The bedroom doorways were covered by curtains that didn't extend across the whole opening, and that fell down in the slightest breeze. It was an uncomfortable place, and dirty. There was no beach at the edge of the river where we swam, only a muddy embankment, and none of us cared to clean our feet before we went back to the cottage to change.

The outhouse, slapped together with slabs of splintering pine, had to be moved every few years. Dark and pungent with lime and shit, it at least had a door that locked so sometimes I went there to change into my bathing suit, away from view, holding my breath.

There wasn't a good season at the cottage. It wasn't insulated so there was no question of going there in the winter, and sometimes the roof collapsed in the early spring when the weight of the melting snow forced its way through rotting beams. One year we went to open the cottage and found the furniture wet and the coffee table bowed like a smile in the middle. The wood was warped and never did break, but ever after it was useless as a place to rest a mug of coffee. My brother has it still in his family room. It is a good conversation piece.

Spring meant blackflies; summer meant mosquitos and my cousins.

My cousins were dangerous people. They drank and smoked cigarettes and hashish while their parents sat in the cottage, somehow believing that we were all really playing Monopoly. They fed frogs to snakes and then put firecrackers in the snakes' mouths. This was the only habit they tried to keep from their parents. I, who loved telling, never told. I sat still at the edge of the circle of sand so as not to be splattered with exploding snake and frog guts.

Anything dreary or dingy or embarrassing that can happen to a young girl happened to me at that cottage. I fell into the river on the long weekend in May and nearly drowned before I was pulled out by the man who rented a room in my mother's house, the man I had grown up hating. Afterwards I sat in my brother's room, shaking, topless, a towel around my shoulders and no one's arm, listening to my aunt scold me again about safety rules and the proper way to get on a boat. Menstruation began, of course, at the cottage, and I was left to deal with it in the outhouse, left to deal with the stomach pain in my doorless bedroom, quietly dreaming of blood.

I was sure there must be a quiet place somewhere, where my elbows wouldn't knock the bedside table, with a large window and a cold sea and a beach, chilled and clammy, that would make the bones of my feet ache. My mother said bare feet would make my period cramps bad but I didn't believe they could get worse. That was before I found out that life offers unlimited opportunity for getting worse.

I read all of Ian Fleming in my room. Would I be the sort of girl James Bond would fall in love with? Was there any question? My mother played cards in the kitchen with her sister and my uncle and the other man. Euchre was the game of choice. Before I could do long division I knew what was trump and how to take tricks and go alone. They were all very fat people who could barely sit comfortably at a table. They smoked thousands of cigarettes. My aunt had orange hair, and a partial plate. Her legs were mapped in red and turquoise veins below her bermuda shorts. Her bifocals were connected by a silver chain around her wattled turkey neck. She favoured my brother who was friendly to her and fetched her lighter. She didn't hit me but she had a slicing tongue. I thought her meanness must have something to do with the strange wiry bits of metal she had around some of her teeth. I was grown up with children of my own before I understood that the metal kept her false teeth in place and gave her sibilants a sharpness that seemed to flay me.

My uncle was bald but he had hair everywhere else on his body. He went whole summers without wearing a shirt. He taught me to play the guitar and to swim and to tuck in all of my shirts. He never said anything when he tried to slip his hands onto my rib cage and up. I never said anything and I didn't stay away either. I thought it might have been an accident and didn't believe it was and I wondered if it might happen again.

I thought that all men matured into a strange shape, alien to the one they grew up with. Up until about their mid-twenties most of the men I knew seemed normal. Slim of hip, more or less broad of shoulder. Delightfully constructed of straight clean lines. Then something happened. My uncle, for instance, and the man who lived with us looked okay from behind but when they turned sideways it was clear that years of determined drinking had altered their shadows forever. Sideways they were gravid with the beer, which gave them huge bellies and C-cup breasts. The disproportion between hips, shoulders, legs, arms, and these huge stomachs made them seem like Martians, candidates for *Unsolved Mysteries*. How did it happen? What was in there? They stroked the greying hairs, caressed their bellies, even named them.

My mother was at the cottage, smoking. She sat beside the man who lived with us and who sometimes kissed her. He was not my friend, though he tried to be. I could never like him or pray for him, even when it was pointed out to me that doing so would make Jesus happy.

A one-eyed taxidermist lived down the road from our cottage in a long low bungalow set well back from the gravel road. The property was surrounded by a mesh fence topped with barbed wire. We believed the fence to be electric and never touched it. If we stood at the gate and waited in the blasting sun among angry deer flies, eventually the doctor, as we called him, would come out and make his slow way down the driveway, preceded by his dog, Laddie. The doctor told us that Laddie, who had one blue eye and one almost pure white eye, was part wolf and part husky. We knew by the way he looked at us that he would eat us if he got the chance; we didn't pet Laddie. We followed the doctor up to the house and shivered in the dark garage waiting for the door to open on a house of wonders. The doctor was an artist with the carcasses of bears, wolves, cougars, fish, owls, butterflies, weasels, rats and snakes. His favourite display was of Laddie the First, a beagle who'd had, it seemed, a much friendlier outlook on life. Our favourite display was at the very end of the room: an illuminated glass cabinet, faintly smelling of formaldehyde, housed the three-headed baby pig that had died at birth and had been donated to the doctor by one of the local farmers. It was small, grotesque, irresistible, with three sets of limpid eyes and three damp-looking snouts, preserved, warm, needy. We couldn't pull ourselves from the pinkness of it.

We whispered in its presence, *Could this happen to a person?*

Sure, my brother said, *I've seen it.*

Have not.

Have too.

Stupid.

You're the one who's stupid.

Am not.

Are too. Haven't you ever heard of thalidomide?

No.

Stupid.

Stupid.

You could have been a thalidomide baby.

What's that?

I'm not telling. Ask Mom.

He always knew everything before me.

One night I had to give up my room to a friend of my uncle's. I slept on the springs of the old couch in the living room, listening to the fist fight outside the front door. My uncle and the man, two fat and ancient men, were fighting over my mother who matched them pound for pound and year for year. It made my stomach cold to listen. Who were these people and why did they drink so much and if they had to drink so much beer, why not wait and let it knock them down instead of each other? Being drunk did not help them. They sounded like my brother and me only stupider, slower.

'You're a lousy son of a bitch.'

'YOU'RE A LOUSY SON OF A BITCH!'

'AM NOT!'

'ARE TOO!'

Followed by punches and vomiting. My mother stayed in her room and seemed to be asleep on another planet. I followed her example. In the morning I poked my head into my room to get my shoes. My uncle's friend was lying on top of my bed, naked with a purple sausage on his. belly. My head was back in the living room before I realized what it was I might have seen.

I thought it would be good to get away from this life. We grew up on Cinderella, but my cousins all seemed to know that she could have nothing to do with them. Woolworth's and the Five and Dime were supposed to have everything we needed. We were all supposed to have been born with a love for the green and blue swans on the tops of our console TVs.

The people up the hill from our cottage lived in their place all year round. Bill had brought Lucia over from Italy after the war but he never actually married her in spite of giving her four or five children, not counting the two from Bill's marriage to Brenda. Lucia had straight black hair, which she cut bluntly at her jaw with her kitchen scissors, and wore parted in the middle. Her eyes were blue but one of them didn't move. I could never tell, when I visited, if she was yelling at me or one of Bill's kids. She spoke with a lisp from having been born without upper teeth. She had false ones but they were uncomfortable, especially when clean; she preferred to do without.

Their house was unfinished: exposed pink insulation between studs, a screwed-down plywood floor. The kitchen's exterior walls were made of gyprock, but between the rooms were only bare two-by-fours through which we could see the wiring and dust at the back of the stove. Lucia was strong. She fed and stroked the rabbits in the shed that were kept until the weather was nice enough to start the hibachi. It was the sort of house where the pet bitch could give birth to a litter of puppies in the dirt basement and live undetected for weeks while we cuddled them. Until Bill finally found out and shot them with his .22, finishing off an afternoon of Labatt's. Lucia cleaned up the mess.

I see her now in the Health Centre, sometimes at the same table as Ambrose. I can't say hello. I'm sure she doesn't recognize me, even if it's me she's looking at. It doesn't surprise me that she's somehow lost her mind, but it makes me nervous, seeing her with Ambrose whose ears are kind of big and whose front teeth, if he's thirsty, protrude a little. I don't want Lucia mistaking him for a rabbit.

I went hunting for bullfrogs with my brother in the marshes around our cottage. He expected me to take the oar and cosh the frog over the head and toss it into the boat. I won his approval through bloodthirstiness. When the front of the boat was full we headed back to the cottage to chop off the legs and feet and then, as if it were a silk stocking, we would peel back the skin. Our mother wouldn't cook them; she said the legs were still alive and would be jumping in the hot butter. We fried them ourselves, adding salt and pepper and ate them on the cottage porch out of the pan, burning our fingertips. We decimated the frog population in that region north of Peterborough. We stopped their voices and ate their legs so the wiser ones moved away. The last few years at the cottage we were reduced to eating chicken legs, which are not as sweet as fresh frog. My children don't know that I was a ravager of wetlands; they think I've always been a responsible composter and recycler. They are gentle children whose uncles keep their hands to themselves while watching Disney movies, and whose eyes dampen when the cat goes over the waterfall, even though they know it lives.

My brother doesn't kill frogs any more and has gone on to live a life I no longer admire, even as he does not admire mine. We used to kill together but we aren't close now. The carcasses of hundreds of frogs are not between us but something is. It could be our mother who died with her legs still covered in skin and attached to her body, uncooked, uneaten, but no less devoured.

I sat beside my mother's hospital bed, swallowing the familiar odour of formaldehyde and decay. Her flesh was disturbingly pink. Her eyes were glassy with pain or with medication or with a vision of another world. I thought, she's free of the man now. Maybe I am too. I wanted him to go away, not her, but she was the one whose heart failed, as though I'd poked the pin through the wrong voodoo doll. I ended up getting rid of both of them. My mother died suddenly. Does anyone ever die gradually? There is no middle ground between breathing and not breathing. She stopped one evening – breathing I mean – and was taken in a slow ambulance far away from me.

The cottage is one of the things from which my new father saved me. His name is Ambrose and he has excellent posture from his years in the military. This is what I noticed first. When I met him he squeezed my arm, my forearm, with a dry, cool pressure containing welcome and distance, my two favourite things. Ambrose was a quiet man. He's much quieter now, but even in his prime, when I first knew him, he had learned about the power of few words. I never was able to stop rattling on into silences. I wanted to save everyone embarrassment because I didn't know that no one was embarrassed, except for me. Quiet people draw intimacies from me and have an unfair advantage in friendships. Larry is quiet, and when I lie on the sheet beside him he feels to me both warm and cool. I trusted Ambrose because he was quiet and because he never repeated anything I told him.

Thanks to his Peggy, Ambrose's house was always clean and because they were both Christians nobody around their house drank or smoked or did dope or blew up snakes. Peggy dusted every day, and vacuumed every other. In the early days of my life with them I would come home from school and she would have the carpets folded back on themselves and the furniture askew; the curtains would be off windows that smelled of vinegar and newsprint, and the sun bouncing off things would hurt my eyes. She called this spring cleaning, which I had heard of in fiction.

On those occasions I was glad that I had never told anyone about my cottage years. I never was so clean before and as I spent more time in their company, it seemed to me that the years before, with my real family and that man I hated and my molesting uncle and disapproving aunt and delinquent cousins and Bill and Lucia, had happened to someone else, or maybe it was something I'd only read about. If I could stay long enough with Ambrose and get clean enough and buy enough shoes and acquire my Ph.D. then maybe I never was that cottage girl. I look like Ambrose used to look before he went into the sanatorium. Our hair is the same colour and I have his oversized ears and narrow, delicate feet. Our teeth are crooked. For a while I liked to imagine that maybe Ambrose was my real father, full of goodness and kindness. Someone I could never hate.

I didn't hate my real father. He built the kitchen cupboards in our house and included a small hideaway shelf for his bottle of Scotch. I heard that he liked Roadrunner cartoons and would hold me on his lap for a few minutes every day after work while he sipped his drink. He died before I was old enough to build a pedestal for him to fall off.

I tried to keep my mother out of the cottage box with all the other memories. I think of her at that kitchen table by herself and not with the other shadows. Whatever the truth was, I think of her as the only person, apart from Ambrose, who enjoyed my company always and thoroughly. I like to manipulate the memories to suit me. I wish Ambrose had some memories to manipulate. I hope that he does and that maybe he's just not saying.

My mother had lime-green sheers on the kitchen door and window. It is enough to admit that she loved them. There's no need to go on about the matching lime-green no-wax linoleum that she hired the next-door neighbour's unemployed brother-in-law to lay the year that she won the big bingo pot. I wonder what it would be like to go back into that kitchen after my years with Ambrose and his wife. My mother's curtains had white felt polka dots and were ruffled priscillas. I probably couldn't find anything like them now. Probably young retro queens out on their own for the first time are scouring the second-hand shops to find lime-green polka dot curtains to put in their kitchens where they will sip mint tea while wearing orange houndstooth polyester bell-bottoms. Those curtains are mine. I want them back.

This was all I knew about old people until Ambrose became one: my mother visited Agnes Lacy two afternoons a week and sometimes I had to go with her though I complained about the raspy sound made by the elastic bandages on her legs when Agnes walked, and about her smell. I stayed away whenever I could. Agnes was too old.

She walked to Agnes's house down the length of Dublin Street in the summer, under the shade of elderly maples whose branches were cut into monstrous bonsai shapes to accommodate the overhead wires. Sometimes I went with her, tripping on the sidewalk cracks as I tried to leap over them. I squished ants under my sneakers. Does God care if we kill ants? I asked her. Does God know about ants? Am I like a God to these ants?

She said, 'I hear you can count backwards from a hundred.'

'Of course I can. That's baby stuff.'

'I don't believe it.'

' I'll show you: 100, 99, 98, 97 ...'

I finished the job, forgot about ants and ontology, as she had intended.

We arrived at Agnes's house. It always looked to me as though it were constructed of pink and grey diamonds. I'd never seen a stucco house before; everyone I knew lived behind brick walls. These diamonds – I knew they could not be real diamonds, however they sparkled in the July sun – seemed an unreliable material for holding the walls of a house. They chipped off easily with a grimy thumbnail. Inside, the floors were pitched at awkward angles so that we listed to the left as we walked down the hall and to the right as we sat in the living room. None of the corners were square. The kitchen was an afterthought, tacked on at the back of the house behind the dining room. Two Escher-like steps down to a tiny sink, counter, and table. It was amazing to me that the house had stood for the fifty years that Leo and Agnes were married. It is amazing to me that it's there still. I wonder if the framed letters from the Queen and the Prime Minister, congratulating them for lasting fifty years before Leo finally succumbed to heart failure, remain hanging on the wall, near the ceiling.

The glory of the place was in the backyard garden, in the two long rows of raspberry bushes, which Aunt Agnes, I had to call her aunt, would cull. I loved the bursting redness of them, but was not polite enough to do better than say, 'Couldn't I please have more?'

Agnes had cast iron dogs and cats to stop doors, and while she and my mother watched *As the World Turns* or talked, I made games with this rigid zoo. I had the animals travel to Busch Gardens and Las Vegas by means of Agnes's velvet souvenir pillows, where the dogs and cats swore true love to each other.

Agnes gave me a quilt made out of her old dresses. She gave me an African violet to look after, which I killed through neglect, and raspberries which I thoughtlessly ate with cold milk in front of the television. She lived across from the high school and assured me that when I finally progressed that far I could come and have my lunch with her. But she wheezed and wore bandagy things on her legs. She was old. Her house was crooked and had a doily smell of lace and old dust that choked me as I got older. She opened a bank account for me with the huge sum of one hundred dollars in it, for me to build upon. For my education. But I loved a boy and used the money for clothes so that I would be more attractive to him. She gave me things I took, while keeping my nose pinched against her smell. I didn't know she loved me.

My mother never lived to be old. Maybe she thought I would spurn her and so got out early. Maybe she wanted to teach me a lesson. Ambrose is getting really old. He never gives me anything any more. Hardly even recognition. But his is a smell that on Tuesday and

Thursday afternoons I hold against my face and breathe in deeply, as though he were an expensive sachet.

I know that what I remember is dubious at the best of times. I construct my cottage and my cousins knowing they are all dead or lost to me in other ways; there is no one to confirm or deny. Ambrose won't say what he remembers. He won't say my name but he seems very happy to see me so I believe he recognizes me as someone important to him, but I'm not really, not any more. Not as important as the kind orderly who gets him ready for bed every night because Ambrose won't let the women on the floor touch him. I construct my own significance to maintain my connection with Ambrose, whom I love, whether he talks or drools or sleeps. I remember that when I was younger he took me to restaurants and always walked on the road side of the sidewalk. He wore a fedora and took my elbow when we walked, took me up the CN tower and to Niagara Falls and visited or called me every day in the days when he was just beginning to lose his mind, while he could still dial and still converse. To tell me he loved me, making deposits to that account against a future of deficits.

Once we were out walking. Ambrose wanted to know if a girl we had met was in the club and I said, 'What club?'

'You know. The club.'

Club. Hmmm. I said, actually, 'Hmmm.' Club. The girl was young, but not too young, walking downtown, face red from the wind. Ambrose and I were out buying me earrings for my birthday. And he giggled and couldn't look up. Then he blushed.

'What club?' I named some clubs. This was hard because I didn't really know the names of many clubs. I said, 'Zonta? Shriners? No. Rosie's not a Shriner. YMCA? Axe Murderers of America? Come on, Ambrose, what club?'

He finally raised his head. 'Is she.' Here he stopped and mouthed the word 'pregnant'.

'Oh,' I said. 'Oh. Ambrose. I don't know. Do you think? How come?'

Maybe he'd seen a bulge in her coat when the wind pushed it against her. He couldn't really talk about it any more.

Peggy would phone me in the morning, not wanting to be a bother. 'Can you help me get Dad out of bed? Are you busy right now?' and I would hop in the car and scoot down the hill and around the corner, leaving toast to burn. I would run up the stairs to find Ambrose reeking of urine in his undershirt and jockeys, perched on the edge of the bed. 'It's time to wake up, sleeping beauty,' I'd say, laughing. 'Get ready for true love's kiss.' Peggy would take his right hand and elbow and I would take his left and we'd pull. I'd pull against Ambrose's weight, his silent determination, and the laughing I couldn't stop when I looked at him, straining against us, wanting to be left in bed. Why was I laughing? What was so funny? This memory makes me happy. It was almost as if I believed that getting him downstairs would cure him, at least for the day, and I knew I was strong enough to do that. I could deal with that. It was as though I felt reassured that anyone fighting with this much determination would live a long time.

I leave my family at home when I go to the Health Centre. Larry sometimes comes but it's easier for him to stay with the children and he never knows what to say. He doesn't like to see Ambrose the way he is.

Ambrose sits through most of his days now and when he walks he shuffles. His stride is lost. The place he is in is called a 'health centre', which is quite a funny name for it. Sometimes I'm sure that Ambrose finds it as funny as I do. We have the same love of irony. There's a chance he may have Hodgkin's disease, or one of the other more euphemistically named cancers. The family has decided against a biopsy and the taking of any heroic measures. If they'd asked me I'd have told them I thought Ambrose was worth any number of heroic measures, even though he's not too clean any more and doesn't make much sense. I tell him he's my dad and I'm his Connie. I told him I got a new job and I was going to get rich and come get him and the two of us were going to Bermuda. That's when he told me I was full of beans and I laughed. Words like Bermuda still channel into his consciousness, as though he remembers riding his rented motor scooter along the shore on the one holiday he spent there. He always wanted to go back.

Remembering how to go to the bathroom is hard for him, but remembering Bermuda is easy. Ambrose used to sing, 'When I was single my pockets would jingle, I wish I was single again,' and a song about Bonnie lying over the ocean, but in his version Bonnie had only one lung due to a bout with tuberculosis. These songs still make him smile, though he doesn't join in any more.

Sometimes I say to him, 'Where are you, Dad? Are you in there?' He doesn't answer me but I like to ask, just in case he really is in there, quieter than ever, annoyed with everyone for talking to him as though he were an immigrant whose grasp of English will improve if we only speak slowly and loudly enough. He eats and sleeps and gets cold, sad, or happy, but I know he's more than the sum of these parts. That's who I talk to and whose hand I hold and whose cheek I kiss. Sometimes he crosses his eyes and blinks like a cartoon of adoration and we laugh together.

The best thing about his old days was curling up beside him on the couch, as though I were small and he were my real father. There is a couch in the Health Centre and if I hold out the Kit-Kat bar at just the right time, he will stop shuffling down the hall and sit beside me while I feed it to him. I can put my head on his shoulder and he might say, how are you, darling, and I might say, fine.

Larry will dig a symmetrical grave for Ambrose. He will use the backhoe to begin with, after he's carved out the grass and rolled it up like a sleeping bag. Then he'll do the finishing by hand. Ambrose believed he'd be in heaven while we were lowering him in the opposite direction. 'Remember, Connie, *"To be absent from the body is to be present with the Lord."'* I want to know where he is now, when his body is demanding only the merest presence. Does God have the rest?

I imagine that I am devoted to him, that everybody else has shut up once and for all about drinks of juice and what's for supper and why are you going to school when you're so old? I imagine taking my books and papers to balance on my lap in a chair beside him, preparing for tomorrow's seminar, keeping vigil with Ambrose. So that if he should open his eyes and know something, it would be me that he knows. I would like to be known again, to visit that place he made for me.

This is what I want: I want to claim Ambrose's body from the authorities. With my tears, these tears I live with, I would wash his feet and then dry them tenderly with my hair. I want to lay him in a vault, roll a stone in front of it, and mourn him daily. When some days have passed, I want to take some scented oil from the shelf above the bathtub and visit that vault early on a misty, quiet morning. I want to be terrified to see the stone rolled back and light blaze within the tomb. I want two angels wearing lightning to tell me he is risen. I want to be the one with the news.

Epigrams

A Smell to Cover a Smell

Connie sat in Ambrose's house where the floor creaks under the broadloom and where his Westminster chimes intone the quarter hour. Peggy was away. Connie watered the plants listening to the pendulum move time. It never occurred to her that clocks should stop. That Ambrose should stop, and so suddenly. No suspense. Like death described by Guildenstern. In one scene you're here and in the next, you're gone.

Connie had a good sense of gone. Both her parents were gone. She knew that gone was gone for good. She liked Shakespeare. Read *Hamlet, Macbeth*. Ghosts appear, further plots, complicate action, expose the evildoer. The ghost of Hamlet's father speaks in iambic pentameter to his son. Hurry up. Get going. Kill your murdering uncle and avenge my death, but leave your mother out of it. Connie was waiting to be haunted.

The funeral itself was fine. Connie sat, impressed with people's ability to condense a life. To make other people laugh at Ambrose's outrageous sense of humour.

He and Hughie had stayed at old Mrs Peterson's house when they were in Toronto for the Easter conference. But they couldn't stand her perfume. Peggy's mother had always insisted that people who wore scent did so because they stank. 'A *smell to cover a smell,*' she said, 'clean people don't bother with such rubbish.' Mrs Peterson was affectionate, conspiratorial. When she had something to say it was always confidential. She stood close, touched and patted the people she spoke to. Bent her head toward them. Her perfume made Ambrose and Hughie gag.

What she needs, Hughie said, is an honest opinion.

'What she needs is a bath,' said Ambrose.

Hughie and Ambrose filled the tub. Then they went downstairs in Mrs Peterson's own house, stood on opposite sides of Mrs Peterson and they put their arms around her shoulders. Blithe. Laughing.

'Now, boys,' she said to the six-foot men on either side of her, 'What can I get for you?' Mrs Peterson was a great baker of sticky buns, sour cherry pies, feather-light scones, the bread of heaven in abundant supply on the kitchen counter, ready for her 'boys'.

They slipped their forearms against the back of her knees and Mrs Peterson quickly collapsed into the makeshift seat of their arms.

'*You boys stop this nonsense!* Alfred! ALFRED!'

Alfred stayed in the dining room polishing his fossils, organizing them by era, neatly inscribing small cards with new information from his library books. He heard his wife, of course. Just as he had heard the water running in the bathroom upstairs in the middle of a Saturday afternoon. Over the years he had gotten used to the smell of dust, of coprolite and shale and newsprint in the room where he spent much of his time. But he had never been able to stop his nose running in Dorothy's presence. He heard her shout but he didn't answer. He sat, smiling and rubbing, scratching his pen across the paper, recording details by the open window. His wife might be less pungent finally.

'Alfred, where are you! Ambrose! Hughie! You boys stop this. You'll never get another biscuit in this house if you don't put me down right now! Alfred!'

Hughie and Ambrose carried Mrs Peterson upstairs and put her, fully clothed and clutching her bosom, into the bath, closing the door on the way out. She was stuck in the tub, her dress and girdle and stockings and oxfords, sodden. She gasped and sputtered and splashed. The two men took the half-dozen crystal atomizers off her dresser and placed them, each one clanking against the other, in a paper bag. Then they took the parcel and went out for a walk. When they came back Mrs Peterson had emerged from the tub and changed her clothes. She had prepared rack of lamb and angel food cake with lemon curd. She smelled like Ivory soap. When Alfred said, 'Everything smells so good, doesn't it, boys?' Mrs Peterson raised her eyebrows but said nothing.

No Good Comes of Fooling

The funeral did Ambrose credit. There were police acting as point men at all the intersections between the church and the cemetery, saluting as Ambrose's hearse passed by. He had lived only in this town. Had fought in the war and come home to fix watches and clocks, to sell engagement rings, to size them on a graduated mandrel, polish them, put them in small boxes for young men who would offer them as gifts, futures contained in velvet. He was not an angry man. He was happy. He loved fishing and, until his diabetes, dessert. He liked to annoy in small ways. He would stir his coffee and put the hot spoon on your wrist. He liked to pinch the soft flesh under your arm, pinning you with his knee against the hardwood floor. If you screamed he got up immediately, sympathetically. Saying, 'That hurts, doesn't it?' The church was filled to capacity when he died.

Connie rode in the limousine with the family. Alice, her sister, was brilliant. She could talk. She found out about the funeral home guy, about his wife's breast reduction and his own concern about his prostate. People confide in Alice. She turns her warm gaze on them and they don't remember common courtesy. They forget the requisite distance of strangers. Even her friends, those who'd felt the force of her eyes a million times and known its frequent unreliability, fell for it every time.

The minister had talked about Ambrose's legacy. To Alice it was energy, joy, and love. To Connie, he said, Ambrose had imparted a sense of the value of the individual.

Individual was not her favourite word. In high school all the individuals were wearing stove-pipes and construction boots when everybody else was wearing bell-bottoms and platform shoes. What did it mean, she wondered. Had the pastor meant that she was the individual? The wacko? The aberration? Or that she could spot one at fifty paces. Which she could. Spot and avoid. Individuals were attracted to Connie. She didn't know why. She hated granola and she liked rare red meat. She thought Birkenstocks must be some man's joke on women. *You want shoes? You want to pay a lot of money? How ugly can you stand it?*

'Ooooh,' all her friends said, 'they're so comfortable.'

They'd have to be.

Connie's best friend, Else, was a quilter. And she sewed her own clothes. And she was a vegetarian. And she didn't shave. Not her legs or her underarms. Connie didn't understand the attraction. Why couldn't Else figure out that she was best friends with a woman whose motto was, 'The mall is my friend.' A woman who knew that grey was the colour for fall, that pleated pants were out, narrow belts in, and that all the blondes were dying their hair brown.

'How can you know this?' Else would ask.

'How can you not?' Connie would answer. The minister said she valued the individual. Had Ambrose taught her that?

The first gift Ambrose gave Peggy was an Indian sunburn.

He shook her hand. 'Nice to meet you, Peggy.' Then he took hold of her wrist with both his hands.

'What ye doin'? Are ye daft? Mother, who's this gleikit Canadian you've brought home?'

Ambrose just laughed and began to twist his palms against Peggy's skin. Peggy shrieked, her mother shouted from the kitchen. 'Ambrose! Leave that lassie alone!'

Ambrose kept twisting until Peggy kicked his shin and jerked her arm away. Her wrist was red. Sunburnt. Peggy's mother came through with the tea in time to see Peggy punch him. Her mother told her not to be so rough with Ambrose who'd only just gotten out of the infirmary.

'*Rough with Ambrose!*'

'Aye, you heard me. He'll no have his proper strength back yet.'

'But it was him hurting me, mother.'

'Ach, come on now, Peg. Don't you know? No good comes o' foolin'. Ambrose'll no' want te come back an ye keep that up. Now.

Come through and help wi'the dishes?'

Peggy was cradling her arm and laughing that teenage laugh that both hails and deflects attention. She stuck her tongue out at Ambrose. She was sixteen, being shyly courted by half the boys in the meeting. Boys who still believed that a shove in the ribs was an endearment, that sticking a foot out to trip girls walking up the aisle to Sunday school was a gift of acknowledgement, a pearl of price. Her wrist hurt. She hated the Canadian. Skinny, big-eared, bug-eyed. Daft. Of course she married him.

Irritation came naturally to Ambrose. Not feeling, just causing it. He liked to provoke small children. His own, at first. Then after they grew, other people's. He would watch them. Catch their eye and then turn his head to look suddenly out the window. His eyebrows would shoot up. Whatever was out there was fantastic. When the children turned their heads to see, Ambrose would snatch their dessert and hide it. Or he'd swipe their G.I. Joe, holding it above his head while the children below jumped and grabbed and shrieked. They launched themselves at him, bumping the table with Peggy's Lladro figurine, the blue boy holding the sailboat. Or they'd knock over the vase, spilling water and flowers, smashing the cut glass. Peggy's mother's admonition ringing in everybody's ears: No good comes o' foolin'.

He would stand in the corner of the kitchen, barely able to squeeze himself between the cold wall and the counter, waiting for Alice and then for Connie to come downstairs in the morning. When they went through the doorway their father would be there, standing like Frankenstein. Sometimes he'd say, 'Boo!' Sometimes he'd snatch them and slip an ice cube into their pyjamas. Sometimes he wouldn't be there at all and they would hurt their necks, checking quickly over their shoulders.

If the Fence Needs Painting

The worst part of the funeral was leaving the cemetery. Connie sat in the cool limousine, driving away, her eyes on the spray of dianthus and ivy on top of the burled oak casket. What she wanted was a transgression of the laws of nature. What she wanted was a sudden resurrection. Her face was a mess, the combination of tears and sweat had defeated her waterproof mascara.

Ambrose had sat quietly in the brown chair, pressing his fingertips together. This was his position for giving and receiving bad news, and for hearing Peggy out. There had been a visiting preacher that morning at church.

'Yea,' the preacher had said, 'verily I say unto you, "Thou art in the world, but not of the world. Come out therefore," saith the Lord, "And be thou separate."'

Peg had sat still. Ambrose beside her felt the pew vibrate in sync with his wife's heart pounding. She kept her hands folded on the wool crepe of her skirt. She looked bland, even interested, but Ambrose knew from experience what he was in for. He knew with what vigour Peggy would mash the potatoes and stir the gravy.

Over make-up.

'Well, Ambrose. You just sit there. A whole congregation, more than half of them women, and he tells us not to put make-up on. He tells us we're not to cut our hair. And you men all just sit there!'

'What should I have done, Peg? Should I have stood up and punched him?'

'Just tell me this. Was there anything in that message of any redeeming value whatsoever? One thing. Tell me.' Peggy uttered this challenge in sharp tones, clacking back and forth across the linoleum from the stove to the sink. The carpet through to the dining room muted her heels till she hit the hardwood floor. Then her black pumps punctuated every syllable. 'Just *tap* tell *tap* me *tap* this *tap*.' The final 'tell me' reached crescendo with the smash of the crooked cutlery drawer, wood screeching on wood. It wasn't a drawer you could close or open if you were mad and Peggy was fit to be tied. It needed a light touch. Day in and day out Peggy would ask Ambrose to fix it, but if he remembered at all, it was only when she was out on some errand or other. He never had a problem himself with any of the kitchen drawers so he couldn't tell which one bothered her, which one slowed her down in her headlong assault on the day. The drawer shrieked closed.

Ambrose tidied his fingernails, dusted the white flakes off his trousers.

'Well?'

'Well, *what*?'

'Well, we *are* in the world, but not of it.'

'Ambrose, the preacher spent twenty minutes – because I was timing him, you might as well know – explaining to us that it was okay to have an eighth of an inch trimmed off your hair and not a speck more. Then he went on to differentiate between the use of face powder, perhaps a misdemeanour, and the application of rouge, which immediately puts us women in line with the whore of Babylon. Now how does he know that rouge is worse than powder? How does he know what it means to be "separate"? And, by the way, that was a lovely suit he had on, didn't you think. Did you notice the way his tie matched his socks? Does the Lord care if I put some pink on these old cheeks, Ambrose, or some on my lips? Do you?'

Peggy stopped in the hall, stood looking at Ambrose who was still seated in his chair. The silence made him look up. She waited for him.

'Well? Do you care?'

'Peg, if the fence needs painting, paint it.'

Peggy painted it.

As He Made Them, He Matched Them

If you talk to Peggy today about Ambrose her eyes will immediately redden and fill with tears. If you can catch her between ladies' meeting, her breakfast club, and her volunteer work, and if you can sit her down for a cup of freshly brewed – and microwaved (Peggy likes it scalding) – coffee, and if you make a comment about how hard it is to believe that he's been gone for almost five years, her response is sharp, unequivocal. She misses him so much.

When Peggy came to Canada on the Queen Elizabeth she arrived in New York. Ambrose was waiting for her on the pier, having borrowed his brother-in-law's Studebaker. He drove her back up to Canada, crossing the border at Niagara Falls. He said, 'Here's where we'll go.'

Peggy hadn't a clue what he was talking about. 'We'll go?'

'After.'

'After?'

'Yep.'

Ambrose couldn't say 'wedding,' much less 'honeymoon'. Peggy finally understood. Driving in the January sunlight in a strange country on the wrong side of wide roads a week before her wedding she understood that she would marry this foreigner and go with him to a hotel room. In Niagara Falls. She loved him. At some point near the end of the war he had stopped putting hot spoons on her hand; she stopped filling his cap with talcum powder. He had held her hand and sometimes kissed her. Had been nervous around her. Had sent for her to come to Canada and marry him. The more she liked him, the smaller his ears got.

Ambrose sat in the lunchroom of the large department store where he rented space for his jewellery business. The coiffed, under-garmented ladies held cigarettes at the scarlet-lacquered tips of their fingers. Cigarette smoke and six different cheap perfumes swirled around the room with the expelled force of their complaints.

'Lazy slob gets home and drops everything at the door. Can of beer, TV, stinking socks. That's my evening.'

'Golf. Three times a week. I say, "Let's go dancing. Let's eat at a restaurant." He says. Listen. He says, and he *means* it, "What *for?*"'

'He won't fix anything. Won't help with the dishes. Won't talk to the kids. Won't look at me when I talk.'

'What were we thinking would happen when we put on that white dress and went to church?'

'We thought we'd live happily. We thought it was love.'

At the mention of the sacred word the ladies became thoughtful, dragging on short stubs, deeply breathing in the smoke. Wiping the ash from their breasts. In the quiet room one of them suddenly looked at Ambrose.

'You're awful quiet down there. Why don't you stick up for your kind?'

'Yeah, Ambrose. What have you got to say for mankind and marriage?'

'What's the big idea anyway? You guys are nice for a coupla months, then you get married and you all turn into husbands instead of men. Barely speak English.'

They waited. Knowing Ambrose went to church. Knowing that Peggy never complained about him. Not to them, anyway. Ambrose looked up from his ham sandwich. When quiet people speak, it's maybe from lack of use or maybe from nervousness, but they seem to be able to make their voices reverberate. The words have more power. Ambrose calmly regarded them.

'I've got one thing to say to you women. *As He made them, He matched them.*' He folded up his brown paper bag in silence and left the field.

Remember Who You Belong To ... and I Don't Mean Me

The thought that Ambrose was in heaven, no longer demented, but healed and more himself than ever before, was compelling. Comforting and exasperating. Peggy felt that measure of relief that the caregiver always feels and she wasn't guilty about it. But she wanted him back. She wanted visitation rights. She wanted the schedule, the responsibility, the laundry, the aggravated corns from the walk to the Health Centre. She remembers being driven away from the cemetery in a limousine, aware of the growing distance. Miles already stretched out between life and death. She left Ambrose in the casket, suspended above an open hole, camouflaged in ribbon and lisianthus.

When Peggy's mother, Isobel, was being courted by her father he would take her to the train station on his off days and talk to her about what it might cost to travel as far as Glasgow, or Irvine, or even London. He would talk about punching tickets and watching the countryside. On their way out the door, Peggy's grandfather would intone a reminder to his daughter: 'Mind who ye belong te, and ah doan't mean me.' Isobel knew her father was reminding her that she belonged to God and ought to conduct herself accordingly. It was one thing to shame your earthly father, another to think about kissing a fella behind the train station in full view of your heavenly father. Peggy's mother said the same to her when Ambrose had stopped larkin' about and appeared to be coming to terms. And both Ambrose and Peggy said the same thing to Connie when she left to spend the weekend with Larry at his parents'.

'Remember who you belong to.' Connie felt a brief thrill. She belonged to Ambrose and Peggy? Really? Finally? When they said, in unison, 'And I don't mean me,' she breathed out. Of course. Belonging to the Lord was something she had grown used to. It ought not to be disappointing.

More than half a century ago, Ambrose and his brothers had once challenged their uncles to a canoe race across the lake. They had escaped tea towels and elbows-off-the-table. Their mothers were miles behind them in houses, knowing nothing. Mothers who couldn't belch, wouldn't fart or spit. They were camping with their fathers who thought boys should learn to move their bowels behind trees and know enough not to clean up with poison ivy. That boys should learn to aim their piss in a stream that arced elegantly and reached as far as possible. On these trips they said, 'I bet I can hit that tree. I bet I can hit that rock. See that robin? Time for a bath.' They shoved each other. Bruised each other with high spirits. Tore shirts that their mothers would later mend with pinched lips.

The boys hoisted the canoe off the truck and joggled it down to the beach, grunting and spitting. Ambrose's father and uncle lifted the other canoe down and eased it into the water. Ambrose stood on the gravel beach, looked around at the broad swaths of blue sky and green leaves above him and at the clear grey water laving his toes. He heard the slip of the canoe off the stones and floating on the slick ripples of the lake. It was warm and still and Ambrose was caught there, held. His father took off his shirt. The few hairs on his chest were starting to go grey among protruding moles sprouting wiry, alien hair. He looked old to Ambrose who would soon be fourteen.

The boys were laughing, piling into the canoe, four of them with lean, long arms and sunburnt backs. Grabbing paddles and gracelessly chunking the canoe from left to right. Ambrose was among them, looking at victory. They would race to the island, a quarter mile away. This is fun, is what Ambrose thought. Brilliant. He looked at the other canoe, at the old men wrinkled, grossly bare with their plaid shirts off.

Somebody said *Go* and the boys careened forward, the bow lifting out of the water and smashing down again while they stretched their paddles, flailing at the lake, driving it out of the way. When Ambrose looked to check how far behind his dad was, he was in time to see him passing, tortoise-like. The old men were casual, quiet, their torsos motionless while their shoulders and arms made long, deep strokes with their paddles, sliding the canoe across the glossy surface of the lake. Suddenly useless to his cousins who were quickly losing, Ambrose was stymied by something fine.

Soon after that race and that day, Ambrose's father got pancreatic cancer and went, as the preacher said, home to be with the Lord. Ambrose learned to be quiet. In his later life, he often regarded the few grey hairs on his own mostly hairless body with an air of satisfaction.

Change and Decay in All Around I See

Ambrose took photographs. He loved flowers. He had no prudence. He loved bougainvillea. The bigger, the pinker, the better. He stuck Peggy among lilacs and sandcherries, in fields with poppies or heather or phlox or dandelions. He got her out of bed to go to the botanical gardens where he would snap frame after frame of tulips and roses and dogwood and forsythia and hydrangea and quince. He put Peggy in for contrast but he wanted mostly the flowers. He loved the delineation of calyx, pistil, and stamen, the camera's ability to put them in your face.

On trips through Scotland he'd get his fill, sometimes. Or it might be too early or too late in the season for flowers so he would photograph old churches and small harbours. He would bring the film home to get developed. When Peggy sat down to look at the photos or the slides she would laugh at him. Of all the relatives he visited, all the people he talked to and went to restaurants with and to church with, there might be a mere dozen photos with smiling, florid faces of familiar people. The rest would be flowers. Peggy beside the flowers, in the flowers, holding the flowers in Glasgow, in Bermuda, along the Hatteras, in Annapolis and Myrtle Beach.

When things were beginning to get bad so that Ambrose couldn't fix watches any more, not even the watches that his old customers would bring to his home, he would say, 'No, sorry. I don't do that any more.' He stopped going to the basement where his workbench was, cluttered with tiny jewels, watch crystals, balance springs, main springs, pinions, escapements, as well as the tools he needed for handling them, the pliers, files, tweezers, ferrules, gravers, and centrifuge. He turned away from the elements of his former skill the way you might turn from the French side of the cereal box. He didn't see the point, couldn't, any more, speak the language. But he would still get up after an ice storm and take pictures of the skeletons of ice that encased the trees. Poster stuff without a homily. Sunshine, ice, silence.

Ambrose started taking the negatives downtown to the camera store to have copies made and enlarged. He would go to the bank and make withdrawals to pay his account at the framing place. He returned to watchmaking once, to cull the old pocket watches and their several parts and hang them on a piece of knotty pine at the bottom of the basement stairs. Peggy's house is crowded with evidence of her husband's determination to keep a record, to hang it on the walls and show it to himself. *These are the things I have seen. This is where I have been.*

There was a meeting. It seemed clear to Connie, sitting alone at one end of the long table with Peggy and Alice to her left and a range of professionals, nurses, therapists, social workers sitting with their pens poised above blank pages to her right, that her father was not happy at home. The meeting was called by the social worker who, upon visiting Peggy in what she called, 'the home environment', observed a puce and aubergine bruise above her right eye, fading now, but it looked like it had been a bad one. Connie liked the distance imposed by the table, the clarity. It seemed clear to her that the disease was progressing, that Ambrose's problems would not abate, but rather increase. If he told Peggy she was empty-headed, if he roughly shoved her out of his way, if he spat his pills into her face, if now, today, he did all those things, intermittently holding her hand and calling her 'Peg, darlin'', then tomorrow what everyone should expect was that it would be the same only worse.

Peggy sat at the table, hearing what the nurse said or the day centre worker, sometimes crying. Her husband had become the subject of a task force, a task, a case requiring management. Alice rubbed her hand and kept her supplied with dry tissue. Each of the professionals on Ambrose's case spoke in turn explaining 'the situation', offering what they believed were options for Peggy to choose. Ambrose could go to the day centre three days a week instead of two. Maybe even four days a week. Maybe his daughters could be with him on other days for a while to give Peggy a break. Peggy listened carefully. Hanging on to their words for dear life.

Connie wanted to speak. She imagined her voice would waver, not because she might be going to cry. But because she wouldn't and she was certain that she should. These, she thought, should be emotional moments, these should be difficult words to say. Instead she felt their redundance. She thought it should go without saying, except nobody spoke. Not the words she had in mind. Other ones:

'What are some of the difficulties?'

'How can we best respond to them?'

'Would three days per week ameliorate the situation?'

These questions came from the social worker who dealt with Peggy and Ambrose. And they came from Alice. Alice wanted to help. Connie's eyes began to ache from staring at the imitation wood grain of the table. Maybe they would dampen and spill tears which would be helpful. She wondered why no one was stating the obvious. She could hardly bear to say it. Everyone down the length of the table had looked at everything else in the room. Some faint breeze, some corolla of dust motes turned gazes toward Connie. The social worker asked her what she thought. Was there anything she wished to say?

It was like answering the question, what is the capital of New York? What is the capital of Mexico? The answers were self-evident. *Peggy cries every day. Peggy is always frightened and unhappy. She suffers migraines of the kind that used, in the days of health care subsidy and a plentiful and content nursing staff, to send Peggy to the hospital emergency room for syringes of Demerol and Gravol. Now she endures the pain because she can't sleep if Ambrose is awake. Never mind the bruises, which nobody knew about until today.* Imagine dreadful minutes accumulating into days, time grinding past while the trachea contracts making it difficult to breathe.

Peggy is small, buxom, mighty. The kind of woman who has always run circles around other people who think themselves energetic. You can rub her shoulders, but you will never knead the tension from them. You will not feel muscle rest against bone. Whether she's laughing or weeping, her back is braced, holding up against the world's weight, against Ambrose's illness, against her double-D bra. She does good works. She has been in many nursing homes where she has visited first, the grandmothers of her new Canadian friends, then their mothers, and, finally, some of them. It has pained her to see them incapacitated, to know, with her eyes stinging and her nose pinched, the ignominies they suffer. She wanted to keep Ambrose out of an institution. She has kept her secret vow that she will look after him at home. Alone in her house she has rinsed sheets, swallowing vomit, saying out loud that Ambrose will go into that place over her dead body. Now that she feels half dead, she's confused.

Connie knew some of this and this is what she spoke. She knew that Peggy was minding the hours like she's the living dead. She couldn't find rest. Connie had bought her gift certificates for manicures and facials, which Peggy presented to pink-coated aestheticians. She assumed a position of ease and raved about it afterward.

But Connie knew that she had not been able to give what she most wanted to buy for Peggy: a few minutes' peace.

When Connie had her first baby, Joy, Peggy liked to say, 'Ach, you don't know you're born.' This took some figuring out. Joy took a long time to be born. Connie, on an epidural drip after twenty-four hours of labour, was not completely connected to reality, but she clearly remembers the doctor's face between her stirruped legs, his drawn brow above the sterile mask, assessing the wreckage below and shaking his head. Finally, he used forceps. Connie heard her coccyx crack. It was awful, but within a few days she was certain that Joy was going to be one of those miraculous infants who prefers to eat every four hours and peacefully sleep in between times, and who prefers a good eight hours' sleep at night. The first time Joy slept all night, Connie woke up at three in the morning, waiting to hear the baby cry. Her breasts were full of milk. The silence worried her. Of course, she wondered if Joy was dead, wondered if she should go and check on her, wondered if the squeak of the floorboards would wake the baby. She decided that Joy was probably sleeping, and that she should accept this gift, and that if the baby *were* dead, she, Connie, would need her sleep for the funeral. This thought made her laugh softly. She lay, expecting to be disturbed every moment, and fell asleep without realizing it. Joy slept through the night from the age of three weeks. She had no colic, no diaper rash, no problem latching on, she didn't cry when she got needles against polio or diphtheria or measles or mumps or rubella. She only briefly looked concerned. She was nice. Connie couldn't believe it. Peggy said, *You don't know you're born.* She meant that Connie's life was too easy. So easy, she could barely ascertain her own existence in the world. She meant that suffering makes us know we are alive.

This is what Connie knew about Peggy's life. Alice didn't know because she lives in Halifax. The professionals didn't know because Peggy wouldn't tell them. They didn't know that when Ambrose is home, Peggy dreads imminent words and deeds. While he's at the day centre, she hurries to the bank, the mechanic, the grocery store, the pharmacy, the post office, the doctor's, the hairdresser's, while the gears in the grandfather clock turn their circles. The brass weights descend; the chimes sound. Peggy races. As soon as Ambrose is on the special bus in the morning, Peggy says, *Only five more hours till he gets back.*

Connie said, 'He will not get better. He will only get worse. That's true, isn't it? And it's bad now. Worse than we knew. I think –' She stopped to look at Peggy and Alice, who didn't look back. 'I think if he can get into the Health Centre now, then he should go there. I think there is no more coping with this.'

Nobody Likes a Skinny Girl

Bosomy women turned Ambrose's head. He was certain that nobody liked a skinny girl and if you asked if he thought Mavis attractive or Corinne elegant his reply was unequivocal: *'Seen better legs on a chicken.'* Ambrose liked women with meat on their bones. Peggy considered her own generous bust more a curse than anything else. She endured the backache and headache, the sore feet, and fought the poor posture that afflicts large-breasted women. Ambrose thought they were great. Ample, inviting, womanly. 'Aye,' Peggy would say, having been unable to breastfeed her children, 'and who would think these big things would be just for decoration?' When called to the table or the phone or the door, Ambrose was fond of saying, 'Chest a minute.' The same Ambrose who mowed the lawn, singing, 'I like to go swimming with bare naked women….' Though he never could bring himself to sing the second line – 'and swim between their knees' – he liked the suggestion of his own rakishness.

The day after Peggy first arrived from Scotland Ambrose took her for a walk downtown. The wind was cold across Allan's Bridge and she was nervous, wondering whether to take his arm. She swallowed, found it difficult to speak. A woman more busty than Peggy, wearing a Persian lamb coat and matching hat came striding across the street toward them, yelling at Ambrose. He looked up from the sidewalk cracks and shouted, 'Ruth!'

Ruth sprang against him, planted a quick, noisy kiss on his lips. 'What have you got in your mouth?' Ambrose's face was up against hers, laughing.

'Just gum. Want some?'

'Sure,' Ambrose answered, and in front of Peggy's staring face, Ruth deftly slipped her gum into Ambrose's mouth before she finally disentangled herself. Peggy was smiling as though this was something that happened in front of fiancées every day at home.

Ambrose introduced them. Ruth said, 'How do you do?' and Peggy answered with equal formality, 'I'm very pleased to meet you.'

Ambrose never explained to Peggy who Ruth was and why he should be kissing her in the middle of the street in 1947 or sharing her gum. Canada seemed peculiar anyway. Too cold, too open. Few quiet lanes, an unsettling distance between folk. Peggy believes the gum exchange was simply post-war high spirits. Alice, Peggy's real daughter, doesn't know what to believe. The story is strange to her, like a Gene Kelly dance sequence in *An American in Paris*. Why is it there? How does it further the plot? But Peggy's adopted daughter, Connie, likes to think of Ambrose as having lived a buoyant, roguish sort of life. The sort of life she lived with him. Where she might once more turn the corner from the hall into the kitchen, first thing in the morning all sleepy and slow, and be blindsided by her father, who jumps out from his hiding spot where he'd been waiting, squeezed between the cold wall and the counter. Where she might feel again that exquisite fright and fury. The sort of life where God's affability seemed evident in the sayings that framed Ambrose's life, that framed his own chronology. One where good *does* come of fooling.

Gifts from the Well-Intentioned

IRIS MURDOCH SWAM in a river that ran alongside the bypass road from Oxford.

Peggy's daughter had given her a copy of the *New Yorker* to read because of John Bayley's personal history about his wife, Iris. Iris swam in her slip. Slipped into the river, having crawled through a gap in the hedge and shrugged off her clothes. But that's not right. She and John swam naked, having skidded down the bank like water rats. Then when they got out, they dried off using Iris's slip. This was before much of what had been her life slid gradually from her mind. Bayley chose his words carefully. Peggy read them carefully. It was a waist slip, not a full-length one with straps and cups for breasts. Flimsy material and not so much of it. Bayley still had the slip, though they only used it once. He never gave it back. In his article, his elegy, it was clear that he admired its stains, how the slip had gone yellow with age, how the blue ribbon around the hem was wrinkled and faded, how it retained traces of mud from their first slipping into the river.

The sudden quiet had disturbed Peggy's sleep. Rain had been whaling against the bedroom windows, hitting the glass so that the noise beat off all the empty house sounds. She liked the storm. She wished it would storm every night. Hail, wind, rain, thunder, lightning. She took them as gifts. She could fall asleep and not hear the furnace switching on, the chunk and whine of the fan, new heat thumping through cooling aluminum ducts. She could fall asleep and not hear the sound of her own solitary breathing. Then the rain had stopped and she woke up cold. She leaned across the cold sheets on Ambrose's side of the bed to the night table and switched on her electric blanket and her lamp. Peggy kept the glass of water and the Imitrex beside her. She popped one out of its bubble and swallowed it. At twenty dollars a pill she wasn't about to take the recommended dose. One would do. She sipped her water and read.

Bayley's work, its evocation of his life with Iris, their lives, is constructed around an organizing metaphor. Swimming in water. In a tributary of the Somme, in a stream farther south. Wherever they found water they swam. Iris liked the water. She swam, as Bayley says, as naturally as a fish, floating, contemplative, weightless. Nearly drowning twice. Peggy had read some Iris Murdoch. Her character, Marian, in *The Unicorn*, looks at a sea that kills people and privately decides, in spite of warning, that she will swim all the same. In *The Philosopher's Pupil*, it's Stella who decides to go swimming because it always makes her feel good, because she's been crying and she looks like a wet pig. Indeed, the fictional town of Ennistone is built on a river and renowned for its healing hot springs. There was something in water that restored Iris to her childish self, that divested her of encumbrance. Part of what they seem to have enjoyed, at least from Bayley's perspective, is the mud. They were often streaked with river mud when they finally, cumbersomely, climbed up the bank holding on to branches for support. They would dry off and talk about the Reformation and the Huguenots. Though Peggy grew up beside the sea, she never learned to swim. Hated having water on her face, unless it was for washing. She never showered, never went in pools.

Iris and John cycled together, tried dancing, went to dinner parties. But it was the swimming. Finding a secret place in courtship and early love. Entering it naked as babies. The daring of it. How it would join you to each other, two dignified pillars of the academic community trespassing, slipping through warm air and underbrush to swim in cool water. Thinking about water made Peggy put the magazine down to go sit on the cold toilet. Her head was clearing. She made herself a tray, put two bits of shortbread on a plate, some milk in the creamer, the pot under the tea cosy, and went back to the bed.

The sheets were green, densely woven no-iron percale, an extravagant gift to herself, chilly and smooth against the skin.

Ambrose's side was empty. For a long time now Peggy had gone to bed alone. It wasn't a huge expanse of mattress. Just a double bed that had really only seen use on the left side, Peggy's side. Ambrose had always wanted a single bed. He couldn't imagine the need for that extra space since he slept every night moulded to Peggy's contours. His chest to her back. Her buttocks to his thighs. Knees and feet fitted.

Peggy would say, 'Och, Ambrose, move over.'

Ambrose would move closer.

Sometimes she would hear sounds in the night. She heard a creak in the hall floor or she heard the crystal plangent in the china cabinet, disturbed by something, someone.

'Ambrose, there's somebody downstairs.' Peggy nudged him with her elbow. He was hard to wake up. 'Ambrose!'

'What?'

'There's somebody downstairs. I can hear them.'

Ambrose might say, 'Go back to sleep, Peg. I'll check first thing in the morning.' Or he might say, 'On you go, hen. Have a look,' before falling asleep again.

And Peggy would lie awake and get a sore head from staring at the bedroom door, longing for a weapon.

John Bayley's attempts to get Iris into the water were engendered by his desire for them to share familiar things. Things that Iris's limbs might recall. Things that might make connections between them in spite of the disaster. Iris or Iris's body could still swim, but not without socks.

Swimming is one of those rhythmic activities like riding a bike. You can do it with your eyes closed. What the mind may forget, the body does not. Ambrose liked to say grace, to give thanks to God for the food he was about to receive, to give thanks to God for his many blessings. Of course, when he couldn't say the words any more, Peggy took over. Ambrose bent his neck automatically.

Peggy was still getting used to being in her bedroom alone. A year after being admitted to the Health Centre, Ambrose died. On a Sunday. Peggy was sitting beside him while he slept. Listening to his breathing. Lulled by the sound of it into contemplation of the morning message at church. Is your marriage happy? Peggy gave happiness short shrift. Her motto, had you asked her, might have sounded like a tautology. Be happy and then you will be happy. To her it made perfect sense. She sat beside Ambrose, listening to his regular breathing, for a while not noticing the decay of its rhythm. The rattle at the back of his throat.

On that Sunday Peggy looked out the window. The grounds of the Health Centre are carefully cultivated. It is, after all, a private hospital catering to drug addicts, vomiters and bingers, alkies from wealthy families. The gardens are symmetrical; there is an agreeable mix of perennial bee balm, delphinium, lilies, sweet William, astilbe, and peonies. There are rose gardens, trellises laden with climbing, fragrant flowers, the thorns indiscernible. There is a slow-moving river at the base of the hill, not visible from Ambrose's room because the tangle of shrubs and weeping willows obscures one's view. It's a place where both Elvis Presley and Michael Jackson are rumoured to have stayed. Where the neighbours pay an annual fee for the privilege of walking their dogs through the grounds. Where they are careful to stoop and scoop. Peggy never had to watch her step on her many walks along the flagstone path to the entrance. Inside, the floor of the foyer is ceramic with marble inlay. The wainscot is raised-panel oak beneath pale blue walls that emit the smell of costly paint, carefully applied.

Peggy had kept Ambrose's undershirts. She had given some away to Alice and Connie who liked to wear them under blouses, close to the skin. She kept his bathrobe, his razor. In spite of her stringent tidiness, she kept a pair of his socks balled up in the bottom of his closet. These were things, when lying in bed or using the bathroom in the middle of the night, at which she could glance.

In the heat of the summer, and in the heat of Iris's Alzheimer's, Bayley struggled to remove his wife's clothes, under which he had much earlier that day dressed her in her bathing suit, so that he could get her into the water again in their old spot near Oxford. There was some sense of reclamation in this project. The crows were there again and having heard that crows live a long time, Bayley wondered if these weren't the same birds that witnessed their earlier bathing visits.

Ambrose got into the Health Centre on an emergency six-week assessment that lasted for thirteen months and six days. They can do that for people in crisis even though it's a private hospital because there are so few nursing homes that will admit aggressive patients. Peggy could not keep Ambrose at home any more. He had been, at first, restless and forgetful. Then agitated and foolish, and finally, fractious and belligerent. At first she argued with him, told him not to be so stupid, criticized his behaviour, tried to embarrass him, the way one might, in front of company, embarrass an obstinate child into his former, pleasanter self. Then he started bruising her. She began locking her bedroom door against him as though she was Doris Day on an illicit weekend with Rock Hudson. He had to go. She couldn't bear that he would leave, that she had been defeated.

The dementia floor is, of course, locked. If you haven't lost your mind, you need a special badge to get in. There is a distinct smell that attaches itself to these closed quarters. Quarters where there are incontinent adults being well cared for, being kept clean. It is not the smell of urine; it is the memory of the smell, something that has been absorbed in disposable cotton, or mopped off a floor that has then been sprayed with disinfectant. The smell of anti-bacterial baths and institutional laundry. Clean sheets frequently changed. The smell of warm, soft vegetables well cooked and poorly digested. And it is sealed in the third floor, incontrovertible in spite of conditioned, freshened air.

In the spring before Ambrose was admitted, he was still able to attend family gatherings. He was quiet. He seemed to like it best if one of his daughters, particularly and for no apparent reason, Connie, sat beside him and chatted. When Ambrose got restless, Connie's husband, Larry, played catch with him. He handed Ambrose his old black leather baseball glove and the hardball and they would stand at the side of the yard where there was the most room, stand eighty or a hundred feet apart and Ambrose would drill the ball into Larry's glove. The slap and whistle of the catch and the toss, the arc of his arm, the straight line of the ball, the automatic gesture occupied Ambrose long past the time when his shoulder must have been aching and his hand, stinging. Beads of sweat would appear on Larry's brow.

He would ask, 'Ambrose, you all right?'

Ambrose's answer came in silence with the ball's return. Larry would exhaust himself.

When he sat down, Ambrose told Peggy, 'It's time to go.'

Bayley writes about a woman who compares being married to an Alzheimer's sufferer to being chained to a corpse, a much-loved corpse. And Bayley is appalled by the comparison. Throughout his relationship with Iris, whose many intimate friendships Bayley had no part in and about which he seems to have had some misgiving, she asked him to think of Proteus, to keep holding onto her no matter what kind of shape she assumed, not to let her slip away.

Most of Ambrose's friends hadn't visited him. Some of them got as far as the lobby of the Health Centre, but turned back because of the scent of fresh flowers on the antique sideboard, or because of the restaurant to the right of the main entrance, or because of the sunny clean windows. Because the place was *nice*. Because the place was nice and yet Ambrose was upstairs, demented. Mental. Incapable of topics, of reading the books they brought him, of comprehending the Bible verses they had prepared to read to him. Bedlam would have made more sense. They told Peggy they wanted to remember him as he had always been, rather than face the absence that he had become. Although of course they didn't say exactly that. They said it was too hard to see him like this, but they said it without a concept of what 'this' was.

Peggy answers her friends when they ask her how she is doing. She tells them that she's doing fine. In order to function, to open your eyes, scrape the wee crusties out of the corner with a clean fingernail, to sit up and swing or drop your legs over the side of the bed, you have to believe that movement from the pillow to the bathroom to the kitchen's coffee smell, out the door to squeeze the kiwis and thump the cantaloupe, scrutinize the cheese and meat, check the eggs (and remember, it's not enough to look because you do that every week and there's always one sneaky egg, cracked in its depression, stuck to the cardboard carton, which can now not go in the recycling because of the dried yolk on it and you're not going to wash cardboard, are you?), and on home again is progress. You have to believe that movement and cleanliness and the structure of meals and errands and laundry and the blessing and curse of conversation is progress. For this belief to be sustained, you need motion, the ability to walk, to wash and dress yourself, feed and toilet yourself. You have to be able to perform these basic activities for daily living. Ambrose was tested for these, the BADL, and failed.

It's one of the tests for mental capacity. Peggy read that scholars have done a capacity analysis of Jesus Christ. Specifically about his decision to go to the cross. Was he of sufficient mental capacity to make a logical, rational determination? The question that the specialists put to themselves, based on biblical evidence, was whether Christ understood the decision to be crucified, to give up his life. Was he self-aware? Did he know what he was doing and what the consequences of his silence would be? They decided that his mental state was adequate for the decision. Not that it was a good decision, but that he was capable of making it. He stood silent before Pilate. Poor Pilate, who kept asking, 'Wouldn't you like to say something in your own defence? How about now? *Now?*' For some things, there are no defences.

First you have to fail the IADL, or Instrumental Activities of Daily Living, which Ambrose also did. Driving, managing medication, handling finances, shopping, cooking, and cleaning. In truth he'd never done most of the things on the list. Peggy organized his pills and put them beside his breakfast plate or his lunch or dinner plate;

Peggy took all the money, did all the banking, paid all the bills. She always shopped at the same grocery store, the one with hardwood floors and big windows, with aisles so narrow that one had to be polite to the other shoppers, to punctuate the navigation with a series of excuse-me's, or, would-you-mind-just's in order to shop. Of course she knew everybody's name. And if the chicken legs, backs attached, had too much skin and fat on them, Peggy would complain to Ernie, the manager, and he would tell the butcher and the next week he would ask her if she'd tried the chicken again and how was it?

There's no mention in Bayley's work of Iris ever cooking. As a writer, philosopher, academic, she was clearly taken up with other concerns. Probably there was a charwoman and a cook. Bayley's concern is with her loss of ability to express herself. Her unfinished sentences, her whimpering. How the two of them communicated for a while using what he calls underwater sonar, bouncing pulsation off one another and listening for the echo. He writes of her anxiety. Of her sudden smiles. The photo at the beginning of the essay, Avedon's photo of John Bayley and Iris Murdoch, taken in 1998, offers a study in black and white of their relationship. Iris, with her trademark scraggy pageboy haircut, wears several layers of clothing. The patterns clash. She looks directly into the camera, half smiling. To her right, Bayley is oriented toward Iris, not the camera. His glasses are pushed down his nose so that he is looking at her over the tops of them, the way parents do, or secretaries. It's hard to read that gaze, its mingling of deference and sorrow.

On Friday nights, when he still had his jewellery store, Ambrose sometimes cooked. Peggy minded the shop while he went home for supper. He read the paper, watched the news, looked at the mail. He turned on the burner underneath the frying pan where Peggy had put three hamburgers. He toasted the buns and added mustard, tomatoes, pickles and mayonnaise. By himself in his kitchen he said grace. Often on a Saturday morning he would bring Peggy her breakfast in bed. He made toast and coffee. He always carved the roast beef and he could stir the gravy. But that was the limit of his kitchen savvy. Ambrose knew no recipes.

He liked to drive. He had always wanted a Buick. It seemed to him the height of a luxury he would never attain while he drove his Matador, or his Reliant, or his Tempo. He liked to get in his car and go, dragging a trailer to Myrtle Beach or Cypress Lake. Peggy would have to pack food, the Coleman, air the sleeping bags, load the fishing gear, sweep the camper out, and stop the paper.

Now that Ambrose was gone, Peggy had nothing to exasperate her any more. She cooked nutritious meals for one. She went to Scotland when she could save enough money. She endured the quiet. She learned to flip channels on the remote, to track three programs at once. Peggy got stuck one night on the Monday movie about a young, beautiful scientist whose father died of Alzheimer's and who had developed a theory about a possible cure. She thought that harvesting the brain protein from big mako sharks and inserting it into the decayed brain cells of an Alzheimer's sufferer would cause the cells to regenerate. No more Alzheimer's. Peggy felt some comfort. If Alzheimer's had permeated pop culture, if they were making shark movies premised on it, maybe her children would have some hope. She couldn't change the channel.

Before the sharks started eating people, in the first ten minutes or so, the movie limped along, establishing the story, trying to create in the audience some sympathy for the gross transgression that will be revealed. The young scientist had secretly violated the Harvard Pact; she had genetically altered the sharks' brains so that they would be larger. Then she could harvest more protein. But she had to do this because of her father dying and all, dying slowly while she had to keep visiting him and answering him, every time he asked where his wife was, that she had died.

'She died, dad,' is what the scientist had to repeat every day that she visited. Peggy couldn't get over the fact that the brilliant scientist lacked the imagination to say 'She went shopping,' or 'She couldn't come right now,' and spare her father terrible pain over news that he would immediately forget anyhow.

Some folk, thought Peggy, *don't have the sense they were born with.*

Also, the scientist's pain about visiting her father, stabbing him through the heart as with a bread knife, impaling him with fresh news of his wife's death, was pain at second hand, reported pain, sturdily reported by *the poor wee lassie scientist* to her investors who were skittish about the fact that a shark escaped and attacked some people, and who wanted to pull out of the project. The acting was wooden. Peggy thought she must have been cast just because she had that plummy English accent. Peggy mildly dislikes the English, feels sorry for them. *Imagine thinking that sort of talking was nice.* But she couldn't change the channel. Not once the sharks got moving. Peggy winced when the probe was stuck into the shark's brain while it was alive.

'Och, but it's a smart wee fish,' she said. 'Look out. That man's going to get it.'

When the sharks got loose, planned attacks, and started eating people, Peggy said, *'And quite right, too.'*

In spite of her hope for a cure for Alzheimer's, Peggy was on the side of the sharks. They were killed in the end, detonated, blasted into bite-size sushi. It was no fair.

Peggy wondered if any of the ladies' auxiliary were watching the movie tonight, or if they might talk about it at tomorrow's meeting. They would make suggestions; they would have opinions. It was amazing how people could talk. Somebody's cousin's wife's brother had Alzheimer's so they knew about it. They could talk about treatments and cures. Shark DNA. Estrogen in Japanese women. Aluminum in underarm deodorant. Of course they were pinning it down. Testing their lives against the possibilities. Comforting one another. Peggy didn't mind. She finished their sentences for them. She put herself in the way of these conversations, even though Ambrose was dead. She remained active in the local Alzheimer's support group. She would look after people, thinking, 'This is just like Ambrose.' She read articles and books. She read everything given to her by the well-intentioned.

She went to bed when the movie ended and fell asleep

immediately, lulled by the wind and rain. It was a miserable November. The gas bill would be through the roof. Much later, in the night's vague darkness, Peggy was suddenly awake. Before she opened her eyes, she knew someone else was in the room, breathing. She could hear breath being released slowly. It was breath so drawn out she could almost hear the pulse, tympanic against her own heart's beating. She cracked one eye open, stared down at the carpet so as not to move her head. She saw feet, running shoes, scruffy ones at that. Those ridiculous athletic shoes made by poor Indonesian children. Not even made of leather any more. The ones her granddaughters coveted.

The feet were turned away. Legs too. Peggy's eyes, now both opened, drifted up to the head of the skinny hooded figure at her dresser, his back to her.

Lord, help me. She kept her sewing scissors under her pillow.

He wore blue jeans. If she tried to stab him in the leg the scissors might not cut through such heavy fabric.

The man was quietly going through Peggy's jewellery box, lifting, looking. He put everything down again. He must have thought he was looking at junk. Peggy was suddenly furious. She had good pieces in there, all from Ambrose. Her ruby and diamond ring. Her sapphire pendant. Her pearls.

Lord, help him. She was hot. She was indignant, galled. She felt under the pillow. The fellow was breathing heavily now. Hurrying.

Unmitigated nerve.

He turned to Peggy. Bent. She felt his breath on her face. Smelled beer. She moved. He moved. She slid her hand out from the pillow, scissors opened. One narrow blade with the precision of an accident sliced his neck. She cut him. And started yelling.

Get out of our house! Get out! Get out! Get out! Get out!

He leapt back, grabbed his neck, screaming.

Holy spit! You're f-f-f-f-f-f. You're F-F-F-F-F. You're FFFFFF! Ucking crazy!

Peggy kicked off the blankets and pushed and pushed with her small strength against this lout. He smashed against the mirror on the wall, banged into the sloped ceiling. She pushed him out the bedroom door and watched him slide down the stairs on his backside like a child playing a game. He was gone. Out the back door, left opened, she guessed, for a quick getaway. All her blood seemed to rush to her toes and she fell to the floor. Laughing. Holy spit? She couldn't even tell him to watch his language. Not in the usual sense. She was screaming with laughter. She was ucking crazy. *That she was, attacking the attacker.* Tears running down her face. Her nose running and shoulders shaking. She leaned against the door jamb. She couldn't breathe for laughing. But there was blood on her nightie. Her palm was bleeding. It must have been the scissors. Keeping them opened. And that poor lad was bleeding, too. And Peggy was laughing. Dying to tell Ambrose. And suddenly crying.

After the police and the rescue crew, after the bandaging and the statement, after the clean-up and the tea, they left. After refusing the hospital again, Peggy finally had some peace.

No. I'm not coming. I have never felt better. I have told you all about that poor fella. He'll be bleeding. He was young and very stupid. I know I was stupid, too. But my late husband gave me those things and I had breath and will to fight.

Everyone left. Even the neighbours, who brought in on their slippers leaves that stuck to Peggy's new carpet, who stood with their bathrobes held tightly against their necks, had finally been assured that Peggy was fine.

Are you not scared? They wanted her to spend the night on a bed chesterfield in one of their homes. They didn't want to leave her alone. They wanted to know if she was all right.

Peggy thought about that. She didn't know if adrenaline was making her feel brave or if she was really quite fine. She didn't know if the Lord had given the angels charge concerning her. Her hands were warm. She sat on the couch, sore palm opened beside her, empty.

She said, 'I'm fine. I will be fine.'

The treat that Bayley and Iris Murdoch had given themselves on hot days in summer was to pull off quickly from a busy highway, often blasted by the car horns of people on important, urgent business, to wriggle through the hedge, following a rabbit through the gap.

Iris didn't like to take her clothes off any more. She liked to keep them on. Bayley, defeated by her determination, was often left with no choice but to allow her to sleep in her trousers and sweater. He lay beside her on the bed, feeling perhaps underdressed in his pyjamas. He kept her company. He stayed with her. But she liked to keep her clothes on, arms folded across her chest, Peggy thought likely, if she was anything like Ambrose. Her protests were gentle, though, not violent. There must be some identity in clothing that made Iris, and others, cling to what they could. It reminded Peggy of the pictures she had seen of Jewish women driven to the gas chamber in the nude. How they covered their breasts and their hair. How difficult it was to see differences among them without clothing. At the river's edge, John Bayley eventually gave up when Iris refused to take off her socks. His wife, a doctor of philosophy, lecturer at Oxford, a brilliant writer, world renowned, stood awkwardly and anxiously in her two-piece 'bathing dress' and her socks. So much of her had slipped that she could not herself now slip into the river. Instead, she watched as a pleasure boat passed slowly by with a young, bikini-clad girl on the deck, perhaps adjusting the straps to maximize her tan. Bayley wrote that both the girl and the young man driving the boat turned to look at Iris and him with a sort of stunned disbelief. He perceived his own impression. One elderly man pulling at the clothing of a reluctant old lady. It is, thought Peggy, a graceless picture, apart from the stunning grace of Bayley's endurance.

Acknowledgements

I'm grateful to Trisha Styles and Joseph Gaça at the Homewood Health Centre and to Dr Richard Davis for their help and insight. I owe a debt of thanks to Valerie Ashford, to Joyce McKenzie, and particularly, to Janice Kulyk Keefer, who was the first patient reader and critic of several of these stories.

There are some debts you know you'll never be able to pay. For their kind support I thank the Irvine family.

Thanks to Andrew and Melanie McLennan for hosting a thief.

Thanks to John Metcalf for his scrupulous care, to Tim and Elke Inkster for their excitement and expertise, and to Doris Cowan for, among many things, a lesson in the subjunctive.

The Ontario Arts Council provided financial assistance for which I am thankful.

I owe special thanks to Rico who fronted me the postage and more.

Several of these stories appeared in print in slightly different forms: 'Clean Hands' in PRISM *international* 35:2 Winter, 1997; 'The Light that Fell Behind Him' in *The Malahat Review* 119, Summer 1997; *The One with the News* in both *The Journey Prize Anthology* 1999 and *The New Quarterly* 18:2, Summer 1998.

Sandra Sabatini is completing her Ph.d. and teaching English at the University of Waterloo. She has been published in *The Malahat Review, Prism International* and *The New Quarterly*. Her story 'Gifts from the Well-Intentioned' won the University of Waterloo Creative Writing Award and the Tom Wolf Memorial Short Story Competition. 'The One with the News', the title story from this book, was shortlisted for the 1999 Journey Prize.

Sabatini lives in Guelph with her husband and five children. She has an MA in English and Creative Writing from the University of Guelph.